WAR STORIES

WAR STORIES

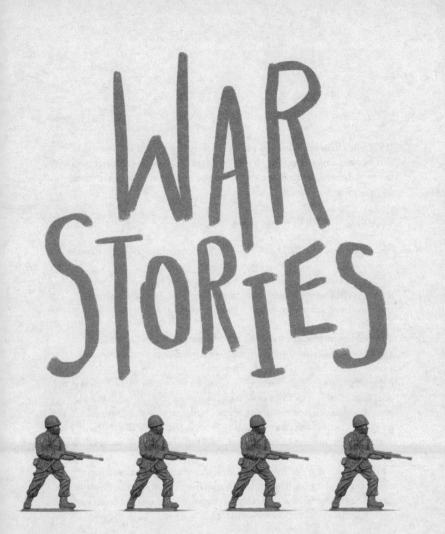

GORDON KORMAN

SCHOLASTIC INC.

Copyright © 2020 by Gordon Korman

This book was originally published in hardcover by Scholastic Press in 2020.

ISBN 978-1-338-29022-6

10 9 8 7 6 5 4   22 23 24 25

Printed in the U.S.A.   40
This edition first printing 2021

Book design by Yaffa Jaskoll

IN MEMORY OF MY GRANDFATHER,
SERGEANT GEORGE SILVERMAN, QUARTERMASTER.
HE WAS A CORPSMAN BEFORE I WAS A KORMAN

CHAPTER ONE

MARLBOROUGH, CT—FEBRUARY 18

The exploding artillery shells blossomed all around him, turning the dark of night into fiery orange day. The rattle of machine-gun fire sliced through the endless booming, carving a spray of concrete chips from the stoop dangerously close to his combat boots.

The soldier crouched in the doorway of what had once been a small bakery. Now it was just a burnt-out shell, along with the rest of the French town, after days of air and artillery bombardment, mortar strikes, and sniper fire.

He was separated from his unit—if there was any unit to be separated from anymore. His entire company had been cut to pieces by a Panzer division as they waited in vain for their own tanks to arrive. It had been how long—ten minutes? fifteen?—since he had last seen an American uniform. Not an upright one, anyway. The dead from both sides lay thick in the streets. The soldier had survived many battles in this war . . . but it was time to face the fact that this one might very well be his last.

The flash came a split second before the explosion. The bakery disintegrated around him, collapsing into dust. At the last instant, he hurled himself out into the street, just as the heavy wooden door frame came down. He was alive—but now he was exposed. He could feel the dozens of German rifle barrels drawing a bead on him.

And then—hope. Rattling up the ruined street came the first of the American Shermans, late to the battle but maybe not too late for him. The soldier leaped onto the tank, scrambling up over the tread to a precarious purchase on the lumbering vehicle's side. There he hung, holding on with his left arm as he fired blindly at the German positions with his right. One by one, adversaries went down—infantrymen, a machine-gun nest, and—

The missile came in with a whistling sound—a shoulder-launched anti-tank shell. He propelled himself free just as the Sherman blew apart in a huge fireball. The explosion launched him forward toward the German line. He hit the ground, somersaulted once, and bounced up, shooting.

"Trevor," came a voice from behind him.

Blam! Blam! Blam! The rifle kept firing, taking out enemies left, right, and center. A German bullet tore into his shoulder. It didn't slow him down.

Louder this time: "Trevor."

"I'm *busy*!" Trevor Firestone's thumb worked like a piston on the game controller in his hands. On the screen, the soldier took shot after shot. Three more bullets ripped into him, knocking him down to one knee. He fought on, bellowing in anger, triumph, and pain. Trevor bellowed right along with him, wrestling with the controller as if it would help destroy the enemy.

Pop!

For a moment, the soldier was frozen there, his face contorted with agony and heroic effort. Then the screen went dark.

"What?" Trevor wheeled around to find his father leaning over the game console, the plug in his hand. "What did you do that for? I was in the middle of this amazing battle!"

"I think two and a half hours of battling is enough for one day," Daniel Firestone told his son.

"No!" Trevor exclaimed in true pain. "Didn't you see how many Germans I was killing? It had to be a personal best! I can't believe you pulled the plug before my progress could get saved! How am I supposed to level up now?"

Daniel looked disapprovingly at his twelve-year-old son. "I hope you understand that, in the real world, killing isn't any kind of progress."

"My guy's fighting in World War II," Trevor argued. "He's supposed to kill Nazis. That's his *job*. Ask G.G. He was *there*."

"You're right, Trev," his father replied. "Your great-grandfather fought in World War II. And I'm sure he would tell you there was nothing glamorous about what he did over there."

"Are you kidding?" Trevor crowed. "He was a hero! He was awarded the Bronze Star—and a medal from the French too. He's always talking about how cool it was."

"He makes it *sound* cool sometimes," Dad amended. "And it was an important part of history. But there's nothing cool about people killing each other."

"That's not what G.G. says," Trevor insisted stubbornly. "Just ask him."

His father sighed. "You can ask him yourself. He's coming for dinner tonight. He'll be here any minute."

Trevor jumped up. "Why didn't you say so?" He ran to the bathroom and began washing his hands.

Dad rolled his eyes. "I've been trying to pry you off that game console for more than two hours. But just the mention of Grandpa's name electrifies you into action."

Trevor toweled off his wet hands. It was true, of course. There was just no explaining it. G.G. was Dad's grandfather, but really more like his father, because his grandparents had raised him from the time his father died. So Dad never saw G.G. as this big-time war hero. Plus, Dad was a history teacher. So he knew about war, but the only thing he ever talked about was how awful it was, and how we all had to pray that it would never happen again.

Trevor wasn't crazy. He didn't *want* war. But World War II was maybe the biggest, most important thing that had ever happened. No made-up story—book or movie—could even come close to it. The forces of evil came dangerously close to taking over the entire world. And the good guys from every part of the globe banded together to beat them back. Everybody talked about saving the planet, but those people actually *did* it. And to know someone who was a part of it—who was really there, helping to make it happen—was huge!

Trevor rushed past his father in the hall. "I'm going to wait outside."

The two could already hear the symphony of car horns that meant that G.G. was coming up the block. Trevor ran out the front door just in time to see his great-grandfather's 1998 Mercury Marauder chugging up the street at fifteen miles per hour, leading a parade of extremely impatient drivers in the cloud of black smoke from its dual exhaust.

Dad appeared on the porch beside Trevor. "He promised me he'd take a taxi. He shouldn't be driving anymore."

"Are you kidding?" Trevor chortled. "He's great. Look how he blocks both lanes. He's sticking it to everybody."

"The point of being a good person," his father explained patiently, "is not to stick it to anybody."

The big car turned into the driveway, clipping the recycling bin and flaking rust onto the pavement. The honking motorists sped by. One of them shook his fist out the window.

Gingerly, G.G. unfolded his lanky frame out of the car. The old man was all legs. It was a point of pride with Trevor that he was built like his great-grandfather. Not like Dad, who was shorter and stocky. At six foot two, G.G. was the tallest person in the family. He always complained that his height had been an extreme disadvantage during the war.

"We'd spend six hours digging a foxhole out of frozen mud, and I was the only one whose head stuck out of it. The snipers used to see me first. You learn how to duck, let me tell you."

Grinning, G.G. stepped onto the porch. He was limping slightly, which told Trevor that the shrapnel in his hip was "acting up" today.

"Hey, kid. What's the good word? Daniel," he added with a nod to Trevor's father.

Trevor beamed. "Hi, G.G.! You just missed the most

amazing game. I was shooting it out with these Nazis, and then this tank came—"

"Trev," his father interrupted. "Can't we let Grandpa into the house before the body count starts piling up?"

Inside, while Dad worked on the spaghetti, G.G. settled himself in the beaten-up old leather chair—the one with the brass nail studs that was kept just for him. In this case, *kept* meant kept away from the garbage collectors. When Trevor's parents had still been together, Mom had tried to put it out with the trash at least three times. Dad had always rescued it. It wasn't the cause of their divorce, but it definitely hadn't helped.

"I finished that new model plane, G.G.!" Trevor called out as he set the table. "The C-54 Skymaster."

"Yeah?" The old man brightened. "Let's have a look at it."

"Sorry—it's at home. Mom's house, I mean." Trevor lived with his mother, stepfather, and twin half sisters, age six. Dad time was strictly on weekends—every *other* weekend. That was his only chance to see G.G.

"I remember when the airborne went out on a drop." G.G.'s weathered face assumed a distant expression, as it always did when he was reliving his army days. "The C-54s flew in such tight formation that they blotted out the sun."

"Wow," Trevor breathed. Once G.G. started talking about the war, the stories just rolled out of him, each one cooler than the last. "That must have been an awesome sight."

"Better than that," his great-grandfather enthused. "It

meant it was somebody else's turn to go out there and get shot at for a change."

"Yeah, but that took a lot of courage, right? To jump out of an airplane?"

The old man shrugged. "Those airborne types thought they owned the world. We crawled through the mud with bullets flying all around us for every inch of progress. And how did they get where they were going? They took a plane."

To hear G.G. tell it, everybody in World War II had an easy job compared with infantry soldiers, which is what he was. The navy—they were out for a cruise. Pilots—nice view from up there. Tank crews—what did they know about sore feet? Engineers—easier to build a bridge than to march across it when the dynamite goes off. Sometimes, it almost sounded like G.G. hated the war. The old man had an explanation for that too. He and his comrades in Bravo Company had been almost as skilled at complaining as they'd been at soldiering. And their favorite topic for complaining was the fact that the entire Allied Expeditionary Force, clear on up to General Eisenhower, was having a sweet time of it, while leaving all the dirty work to them.

"Come on," Trevor chided his great-grandfather. "The airborne were heroes too. They were taking enemy fire when all they could do was hang there while their parachutes came down."

"I suppose," G.G. conceded. "The Germans shot at everybody, not just us. Come to think of it, the whole war would have been a lot better without them messing it up—them and their Third Reich."

The two laughed while, in the kitchen, Trevor's father shook his head, half-amused, half-disgusted. This was the way their conversations always went—war, war, and more war. Sometimes he felt like he should put a stop to it. Trevor's interest in World War II was turning into a full-blown obsession. He played video games about it, read books, watched movies, built models. Both his rooms—at his mother's house and here too—were plastered with posters commemorating military units and major battles. Where were the sports heroes? The TV and movie stars? Was it natural for a twelve-year-old kid to be so totally engrossed in something that glorified death and destruction?

On the other hand, he was thrilled that Trevor had a real relationship with his great-grandfather. After all, what did a twelve-year-old boy have in common with a ninety-three-year-old veteran? It was a *good* thing—in a way. And the reason it worked was that World War II was all Trevor ever wanted to hear about. And Private First Class Jacob Firestone of Bravo Company had plenty to say on the subject.

"Dinner's ready." Trevor's father set the bowl of spaghetti and meatballs on the table. "One request tonight: Can we at least be done with our salads before anyone mentions the word *grenade*?"

Trevor rolled his eyes. "Dad—you're insulting G.G."

The old man took his place at the table. "Don't worry about me, Trevor. I don't insult so easy. You couldn't insult me if you—"

"Dropped a grenade in your pants?" Trevor finished.

G.G. shot him an appreciative grin. "Good one!"

Dad sat down with a sigh. "You two. Eighty-one years separating you, and you're both the same kind of idiot."

Trevor beamed. Having anything in common with his great-grandfather was okay with him—even idiocy. But he did his best to hold off on the war talk until they'd started on the spaghetti.

Spaghetti was G.G.'s favorite food, because during his deployment in Europe, it was "the only thing those slop-slingers in the kitchen couldn't turn into latrine runoff."

Trevor cackled his appreciation. That was another thing he admired about the war. Soldiers were great at cracking jokes.

His father made a face. "Can we please talk about something else?"

The old man pulled a piece of paper from his pocket and began to unfold it. "This letter came in yesterday's mail. It's from the village council of Sainte-Régine."

"Sainte-Régine?" Dad repeated.

G.G. shrugged. "Some one-horse town in France. Our unit passed through there back in forty-four."

Dad took the letter from his grandfather and scanned it. "According to this, you didn't just pass through. You fought a battle there and liberated the place!"

"What?" Trevor was up like a shot, reading over his father's shoulder. It was true. PFC Jacob Firestone of the United States Army (Retired) was the last surviving participant of the Battle of Sainte-Régine. That coming May, in commemoration of the seventy-fifth anniversary of victory in Europe, the village was holding a celebration of its liberation from German occupation. And they were inviting G.G. to be the guest of honor.

Trevor was bursting with pride. "Wow—it's like the whole town wouldn't even be there if it wasn't for you."

G.G. was modest. "I'm sure some other unit would have turned up if we'd decided to sleep in that day."

Dad set the letter down on the table. "It's a real honor. It's a shame you have to miss it."

Trevor was horrified. "Why would he miss it?"

"France isn't exactly around the corner," his father explained. "It's just not practical for a man his age to make a trip like that."

"But he *has* to go," Trevor pleaded. "He's the only guy from the battle still alive! There's nobody else left for those people to thank."

Dad tried to be patient. "Think about Grandpa. Does he ever like people to make a big fuss over him? You know he doesn't. He doesn't visit the monuments or go to the reunions. He refuses to be honored in the Memorial Day parade. He won't even look out the window when it passes by his house. Believe me, the last thing he wants to do is take a trip to France."

"But Dad—"

"If you two knuckleheads are through deciding what I want," G.G. interrupted, "maybe you'd like to hear my take on all this."

Grandson and great-grandson turned to face the old man.

"I'm going," he announced.

Trevor launched into a victory dance.

"Be reasonable," Dad urged his grandfather. "Don't you realize what a strain this trip would be on you?"

"I made it once before," the old man snapped back. "With a fifty-pound pack on my back and people shooting at me."

"You were eighteen years old!" Dad argued.

"Seventeen. I lied about my age at the recruiting center. People said they'd never take me, but I proved them wrong. Just like you're wrong now."

Daniel Firestone stood his ground. "Grandpa, I just can't let you make a trip like this alone."

His grandfather scowled at him. "Who said anything about being alone?" He grinned at Trevor. "Ever been to France?"

Trevor's jaw fell open halfway to his knees.

CHAPTER TWO

SAINTE-RÉGINE, FRANCE— SEPTEMBER 12, 1944

"In my next life, I'm coming back as a general."

His rifle leaning against a tree trunk, Private Jacob Firestone took a nervous bite out of an apple he'd just plucked from a low branch.

It got a short laugh from his companion, PFC Beau Howell. "How do you figure that?"

"You think Eisenhower is standing in the mud up to his ankles, eating green apples for breakfast?" Jacob went on. "You know what Sainte-Régine is to him? A dot on a map."

"Not just a dot, High School," Beau reminded him. "A dot between us and Nazi Germany. And it's our job to go get it for him."

Like most of the soldiers of Bravo Company, Beau was only a few years older than Jacob. But when those few years were the difference between twenty-one and seventeen, it was easy to see how Jacob often felt like a boy among men. They called him High School because the overall opinion was that high school was where he belonged, safe and sound. Jacob didn't agree. But there were moments—when the shells were bursting and the tracer bullets flew by so close that they sounded like lethal mosquitoes chirping past his ear—that high school seemed like a pretty good deal.

He didn't regret it, though. Not for a second. He'd lied about his age because this was where he knew he belonged. His country didn't need him after graduation; it needed him *now*. It had needed him at Omaha Beach on D-Day; it had needed him on the deadly, agonizing slog through the hedgerows of Normandy; it had needed him for operations with names like Neptune, Overlord, and Cobra. And it needed him today for the Battle of Sainte-Régine.

So far, there was no such thing as the Battle of Sainte-Régine. But the next few hours should take care of that.

"It's not about the mission," Jacob went on around a mouthful of sour apple. "It's about what job you do. I could wake up in some posh HQ, take a hot shower, put on clean, dry socks, point to a dot on the map, and say, 'I want that.' Then my part's over, and some poor platoon or company or battalion has to go out and get it for me."

"That's us," Beau observed, checking his rifle to make sure it was fully loaded. Not that he hadn't checked five minutes ago. And five minutes before that.

"Right?" Jacob added. "It would almost be funny except that some of us are going to buy it today."

Jacob wasn't sure about other units, but in Bravo, almost no one ever talked about dying. It was always "buying it." You couldn't let yourself think about things like that, or you'd be too scared to move. Jacob had seen that too—men so terrified they were frozen in place, incapable of putting one foot in front of the other, even to run away. He had no explanation for why he wasn't one of them. The fear was 100 percent real, the danger even more so. Why one soldier got shot—or blown up, bayoneted, crushed by debris—was the luck of the draw. Of the 172 members of Bravo Company who'd hit Omaha Beach on the morning of June 6, only 51 were part of the unit poised to attack Sainte-Régine. Of those 121 casualties, nearly half had "bought it."

Jacob picked another green apple and Beau whacked it out of his hand with the butt of his rifle.

"Stop eating those things, High School. They'll turn your guts to water. Bad enough we have to fight for this Podunk town. You don't want to lead the charge looking for a bathroom!"

"I'm hungry! You can't live on canned Spam—"

That was the end of all conversation. Behind them, the American field artillery opened up, pounding the tiny village a little more than a kilometer up the hillside. Jacob had gotten used to a lot of things in this war; he'd never get used to the noise. No matter how far away the guns happened to be, it always seemed like the explosions were right inside your head. The concussion waves battered you through the air, and there was no place to hide. The scream of the shells overhead sent shivers down your spine. The only thing worse was being in the target zone where the shells detonated. Jacob had experienced that too, huddled in a foxhole, making deals with God. He already owed God about two hundred years of good behavior just to have survived this far.

It was probably only about ten minutes, but while it was going on, Jacob lost track of time. In the roaring/screaming/pounding of it, he very nearly lost track of his boots on the ground and his body plastered up against the tree. He had endured much worse before—hours of bombing, enough to reduce whole towns to mounds of rubble. Then it was over, and the sudden absence of noise was almost as jarring as the noise itself.

Still deafened by the racket, he didn't hear the order to move out. Instead, he was swept along with everyone else. A hand reached back, grabbed him by the field jacket, and hauled him forward. Beau—they always stuck together going into battle, as if each was the other's lucky charm. Maybe it was true. They had gotten each other this far. Other friends hadn't been so lucky.

Soon sweat was stinging his eyes and bathing his body. It wasn't hot, but fifty pounds of equipment made your uniform an instant steam room. That was another thing about war, besides the noise, pain, death, destruction—it smelled bad too.

About fifty meters to the left, along the single road that cut through the trees, the first Sherman tank lumbered up the slope. That was what made the invasion of Sainte-Régine more complicated than it should have been. Vast apple orchards surrounded the village, the mature trees planted so close together that no vehicle could get through. For the tanks, trucks, half-tracks, and jeeps of the mechanized army, there was only one way in: this road.

A sergeant emerged from the tank turret and grinned at the

infantry slogging through the orchard. "Enjoying the walk, gentlemen?"

Soldiers pelted him and the tank with fallen apples. Months spent shoulder to shoulder, fighting for their lives, had turned Bravo Company into a tight-knit family. Compared to the bonds they had forged with one another, the men of the armored unit were strangers.

"What's he so happy about?" Beau grumbled.

"You'd smile too if you had thirty-three tons of tank protecting you," Jacob commented, sidestepping a low branch.

His hearing still deadened by the booming of the American guns, Jacob didn't notice the incoming shell until it was too late. Some of the men flattened themselves to the ground, but Jacob could only watch as the round screamed into the Sherman and detonated. The concussion of the blast knocked him to his knees. By the time he looked up again, the smiling sergeant had been replaced by a pillar of flame spewing from the hatch.

"Medic!" Jacob rasped, scrambling toward the burning tank. "Med—!"

That was all he got out before a second, even more fiery explosion enveloped the Sherman as the gas tank blew. Jacob stared in horror. No need for a medic now. The five men of the tank crew had surely bought it.

A second Sherman came up behind what was left of the first. *This* commander wasn't grinning. His face was all business as he shouted instructions to the crewmen below him. Carefully, the second tank tried to nudge the flaming iron husk out of the way so it could pass on the narrow road.

No one missed the scream of the incoming shell this time. Jacob was flat on his face when it exploded just a few meters short of its target. If the burning remains of the first tank hadn't slowed down the second, it would have been a direct hit. The second tank roared into action, trying to drive around the block in the road. But the space was too narrow, and the left track bumped into a tree. The tree bent, its roots tearing up through the muddy ground.

Boom! Another shell struck, blowing the right track clean off. One by one, the five members of the crew scrambled out of the hatch. The last of them hurled himself free just as the second Sherman burst into flame.

By now, the infantry advance had ground to a halt. Everyone was staring at the spectacle of the two burning tanks.

"Keep moving!" Lieutenant McCoy exhorted his soldiers.

With the column of armor hung up on the road, Bravo Company had little interest in advancing. The last thing the soldiers wanted was to take on Sainte-Régine's defenses with zero tank support and nothing but the rifles in their hands.

"Let's *go*!" McCoy bawled.

Jacob felt the perspiration inside his uniform turn to ice. It had been information from *him* that had led to the plan to take out the big German gun that menaced everything on the road into Sainte-Régine. McCoy and Captain Marone, the company commander, had trusted him. What had gone wrong?

The firefight began in earnest. Bullets whined through the orchard, thwacking into tree trunks and singing past Jacob's ears. The illuminated tracer rounds glowed like lethal lightning bugs, even in broad daylight. Answering fire came from Bravo Company. Jacob flopped onto his belly, raising a splash of mud into his face. Desperately, he wiped his eyes clear, scanning for the enemy. There were figures darting from tree to tree, armed men coming at him.

He fired in their general direction—there was no time to aim and shoot. A grunt of pain and one of the shadows went down. Jacob had no idea whether or not it was his bullet that had done the job. There were too many shooters; too many targets. The moment was total chaos.

Sprays of heavy-caliber machine-gun fire ripped through the trees. Apple-laden boughs came raining down on Bravo Company. Cries of *"Medic!"* rang out through the American ranks.

On the road, an enormous army bulldozer was trying to clear the debris of the two burning Shermans when another artillery blast came screaming down from Sainte-Régine. With a clang so loud it could be heard over the explosion, the shell slammed into the huge blade and went off, mangling it like it was made of paper. The dozer hung there, unable to gain any traction, the twisted metal holding its tracks above the pavement.

Jacob's attention was torn away from the drama on the road by an explosion overhead. A mortar shell detonated in the treetop above, dislodging a huge branch. It dropped, striking Beau across the back, sending him sprawling.

It should have taken a crane to lift the gigantic bough off the fallen GI, but scrawny seventeen-year-old Jacob managed it in one frantic effort. Two German bullets ripped into the wood, but he didn't let go of the branch until it was clear of his fallen friend.

"Beau—don't be dead!" Jacob shouted. "Don't you dare be dead!" He dropped to his knees and rolled Beau over. It took almost as much energy as moving the heavy bough. But it was worth it to see Beau's eyes flutter open.

Beau was dazed and very pale. "Tell General Eisenhower I'm ready for that shower now."

Truly he was. If the ground hadn't been so wet and muddy, the blow might have squashed him like a bug. That was what saved him—that and the fact that his heavy pack had absorbed the brunt of the branch's weight.

"I'll tell him," Jacob promised shakily. "As soon as we get out of this orchard!"

Two medics approached on the run and began to load Beau onto a stretcher. Watching them work, Jacob realized for the first time that the orchard was suddenly quiet.

"What's going on?" Jacob hissed. "Why has the shooting stopped?"

"The Germans are falling back toward the town," the lead medic explained. "We've got orders to pick up the wounded before we press on."

As if on cue, Lieutenant McCoy bellowed, "Move out!"

On the road, the disabled bulldozer took another hit, dislodging the blade completely.

"Looks like you got the short end of the stick, High School,"

Beau commented in a weak voice. "I'm going on vacation and you're still on the clock."

Jacob tried not to let his friend see his fear. Bravo Company would never be able to take the town without tank support.

In other words, if the plan to silence that German gun failed, the attack force was doomed.

CHAPTER THREE

MARLBOROUGH, CT—MARCH 29

Trevor's mother was definitely not a fan of plucking her son out of school and, as she put it, "letting him skylark all across Europe with his father and great-grandfather."

"Come on, Julia," Daniel Firestone reasoned. "How many opportunities is a twelve-year-old going to get for a fantastic trip like this?"

His ex-wife stood her ground. "He'll be missing three weeks of school. How can that be good for a B-minus student?"

"You forget that I'm a teacher," Daniel reminded her. "I'll be with him every step of the way. I'll make sure he keeps up. And remember, there's more to education than what happens in a classroom. This will be a kid who's fascinated with history walking in the footsteps of the real thing."

"Give me a break, Daniel. Trevor doesn't care about history. He's just obsessed with your grandpa's larger-than-life war stories—which, by the way, get even less believable over the years. Every time he tells them, a few more buildings get blown up, and the branch he lifted off his buddy weighs an extra hundred pounds. That's not history; that's superhero comics."

"Okay," Daniel conceded. "The war stories are a little over-blown. Grandpa's ninety-three now. He probably doesn't remember as well as he used to."

"Are you joking? Your grandfather's too ornery ever to for-get anything. He remembers the first waiter who overcharged him for coleslaw in 1940. There's nothing wrong with his memory. The stories are over-the-top because he knows that's what Trevor wants to hear. Our son doesn't love history. He loves explosions."

"He doesn't love explosions—"

"Really?" Trevor's mom swung open the door to his bed-room. Explosions of all shapes and sizes shone down from the posters on the wall—war scenes depicting detonating bombs, tank battles, aerial dogfights, torpedo strikes, V-2 rockets, gre-nades going off, flamethrowers, and artillery barrages.

A suitcase lay open on the bed and Trevor stood by the dresser, selecting underwear and socks. Kira and Kelsey—his six-year-old twin sisters—were circling the room, each waving a World War II model fighter plane, whooping loudly and yell-ing, "Blam! Blam! You're dead!"

"No, *you're* dead!"

"Girls!" Their mother was horrified. "What are you doing?"

"War!" Kelsey crowed.

"Just like Trevor!" Kira added.

The girls ran off under their mother's stern eye. Then she transferred her disapproving gaze to her son.

Trevor shrugged. "It's not my fault they like playing with my stuff."

His father changed the subject. "A little early to be packing, isn't it? The trip isn't for nearly a month."

"And it hasn't been decided yet if you're going," his mother added. "You're very young, you know. Europe will still be there when you don't have to take three weeks out of your education."

"But this could be my only chance to go with *G.G.* We've got it all planned out to retrace his steps exactly from 1944! From basic training in Georgia, to England for staging, and across the English Channel for the invasion of Normandy on D-Day!"

"It's the first I'm hearing about Georgia," Daniel mumbled when his ex-wife shot him an accusing look.

"It's going to be *so awesome*," Trevor pleaded. "It would be great to see these places anyway, but to be there with G.G., who could tell me exactly what it felt like—that would be the best thing in the world. Plus, we're going to Reims for the seventy-fifth anniversary of V-E Day. That's where the official surrender was signed, you know. And before that, G.G. is going to be the guest of honor in the French village he liberated from the Nazis!"

"He didn't do it all by himself," his father reminded him. "The rest of the army was there too."

"Well, yeah," Trevor admitted. "But he's the last survivor of the battle. He's a hero in that town! You should see the Sainte-Régine Facebook page—they've got his picture all over it to get people psyched for the ceremony!"

Daniel cast him a crooked smile. Trevor had shown him

the Facebook page—but Trevor didn't speak French. There was a long list of comments from villagers. Most were expressing their excitement about the ceremony and the chance to honor the last surviving hero of Sainte-Régine. But one post, buried in the middle of the stack, was not quite so friendly. It translated to: *Jacob Firestone is no hero and is not welcome here.* It also said *Vive la Vérité*, which meant *Long Live the Truth.*

Oh well; there was always one discontented crab in every group. Grandpa would surely understand. More often than not, that discontented crab was Grandpa himself. Still, it bothered Daniel that someone in Sainte-Régine wasn't quite so welcoming as everybody else.

"It's important, Julia," Daniel said in an undertone. "You know me. I take the war stories with a grain of salt just like you do. But Grandpa's ninety-three—he isn't going to be around forever. This honor could be his last hurrah. Trevor should be there to share it. We can work on the explosions some other time."

Trevor's mother thought it over. "I guess you're right. But *you're* making the phone calls to his school."

Trevor homed in on this like a bat using echolocation. "So I can go?" He threw his arms around his mother and hugged her. "The girls can use all my stuff while I'm gone. I promise!"

Julia took in the arsenal of lethal military hardware cluttering every surface in the room. "That's okay. I'll keep them busy so they don't—uh—miss you too much."

CHAPTER FOUR

NEW HAVEN, CT, RAILWAY STATION— JULY 23, 1943

Jacob slapped three pennies onto the counter and waited while the clerk carefully tore a single postage stamp off an entire sheet.

He licked the back and affixed it to his letter. Ma and Pa would have this tomorrow, or maybe the next day. They'd be upset—or maybe not. It was no secret how determined he was to enlist in the army.

That was what had brought him to New Haven. The recruiting center in his hometown never would have taken him. Everybody there knew he was underage. But the sergeant here in New Haven wasn't too fussy about the rubbed-out area on his birth certificate—the part where 1926 had been doctored to look a lot like 1925. The center was packed to the rafters, and they were running volunteers through physicals as fast as they could stamp 1-A on the exam forms.

The loudspeaker, crackling with static, was almost impossible to make out, but Jacob knew they were calling his train—the one to New York City and Washington, DC, where he'd catch a connection south to Georgia for basic training. He swung his overstuffed duffel over his shoulder—he had written *FORT BENNING OR BUST* on the canvas in splotchy ink. The bag felt light, but for some reason, the letter had gotten a lot heavier, as if the stamp had added a lead weight.

He hated to do this to Ma and Pa. He was their only son. But how could he ignore his country's call? Across the ocean, the fate of the human race was being decided. How could he sit in English class, reading Shakespeare, when his fellow Americans were risking their lives half a world away? He held the letter out toward the mail slot—

And froze. Had he said everything he needed to in the letter? Had he apologized to his parents? Promised to be careful? Told them he loved them?

A train whistle blew. Something was leaving—*his* train! If he didn't get to Fort Benning on time, he'd be AWOL before his army career had even started!

Panicking, he dropped the envelope in the slot and darted for track six on the dead run. He scrambled down the stairs, where an appalling sight met his eyes. His train was already on the move.

He sprinted across the concrete, the heavy duffel pounding against his back with every flying step.

"Hey!" he panted. "Wait for me!"

Just before he ran out of platform, a conductor at the door of the very last car reached out and hauled him and his bag aboard.

Weak with relief, Jacob slumped against the steps, too winded to gasp out a thank-you.

The conductor read his mind. "Don't thank me," he said. "Someday you'll probably wish you'd missed this train."

Still beyond speech, Jacob shook his head vehemently, imagining the adventure that lay ahead.

CHAPTER FIVE

MARLBOROUGH, CT—APRIL 21

The bag was ancient, faded khaki, the canvas reinforced by duct tape in several places. The ink had faded over the decades, but the message was still legible: *FORT BENNING OR BUST.*

Daniel entered his grandfather's apartment and gawked at the battered duffel, which was sitting on the hall table.

"Grandpa, you've still got that old thing?"

"We old things like to stick together," Jacob replied, stubborn and a little proud. "This bag saw me through the whole war. I even zipped myself into it a few cold nights in the winter of forty-four. It earned the right to make this trip."

"You're *bringing* it?" Daniel was horrified. "You have luggage."

"Not like this," the old soldier shot back. "I could never zip myself into that newfangled nylon monstrosity with a separate compartment for every sock. And the *wheels*. That's why they call it luggage. You *lug* it. You don't *roll* it."

His grandson sighed. "And you don't think it'll fall apart halfway to France?"

Jacob snorted. "This bag was in a transport truck that took a direct hit with an eighty-eight-millimeter shell. Look at it—not a scratch."

"And the duct tape?"

"Marvelous stuff. Never could have won the war without it." The old man stuck out his jaw. "Is that why you're here—to criticize my packing?"

"Sit down, Grandpa. I have to show you something." Daniel followed his grandfather to the couch and settled himself beside him. He pulled out his phone. "I've been following the village of Sainte-Régine's Facebook page—"

"Let me tell you right now that I don't do Facebook or Nosebook or any-other-part-of-the-body-book. And I don't tweet. I'm not a bird. I don't need any fancy gadget to know about Sainte-Régine."

"Here's one thing you might not know about Sainte-Régine," Daniel said seriously. "Not everybody there thinks you ought to be invited back for this ceremony."

The old man shrugged. "There are always a couple of cranks."

"I thought so too. At first. I've been following this page ever since we bought our plane tickets. Most of the town is excited to welcome you. But there's this group. They call themselves La Vérité—it means The Truth."

"I know what it means," his grandfather put in irritably. "I was in France, you know. I walked across most of it."

"But listen to this"—Daniel read from his phone screen—"*Jacob Firestone does not deserve to be honored. He has French blood on his hands.*' Grandpa, what do they mean by that?"

"It's simple," the old soldier explained. "France had already surrendered when the Germans walked into Sainte-Régine, so the occupation happened without a fight. But when we liberated it, we had to blast the Germans out. So they came in peacefully and we had to practically level the place. Is it really so surprising that a few wing nuts came to the conclusion that we were the bad guys? Especially since whoever's writing these so-called comments probably wasn't even born when our boys did what we had to do."

"Some of these posts are downright threatening," Daniel persisted. "'*Stay in America, Jacob Firestone.*' Or this one: '*Sainte-Régine will never forgive you.*' If you still want to go, I'll go with you. But remember, we're going to have Trevor with us. I'm worried about bringing him into this."

Jacob chuckled. "If you plan to tell Trev he can't come on the trip, then you're a braver man than I am. That'll take more courage than I ever showed in Europe."

"Of course I don't want to spoil this for Trevor. I've never seen him so excited about anything. But this sounds ugly. Maybe even dangerous."

The old man's eyes took on a faraway expression. "If this is the past catching up to me, so be it. I've been carrying it around for seventy-five years."

His grandson was alarmed. "What's that supposed to mean?"

"You're always accusing me of making war look too glamorous to the kid," Jacob challenged. "Well, this is his chance to see exactly how glamorous it wasn't. Don't get me wrong— those experiences made me the man I am. A boy Trevor's age can't imagine the feeling that you're a part of something so enormous—a whole world pulling out all the stops to save itself from disaster. Glamorous? Not even a little bit. But worth-while? Ask anybody who was there."

Daniel took a deep breath. "All right, Grandpa. I'm going to trust you that everything's under control. You've never steered me wrong. When Dad died and Mom and I moved in with you and Grandma, you kept me focused and got me through high school and college. I know you've got Trevor's best interests at heart too."

As usual, Jacob had no interest in the emotional side of things. World War II had squeezed that out of him. "Let's just enjoy this trip," he said gruffly. "It's going to be a hoot!"

CHAPTER SIX

LAGUARDIA AIRPORT, QUEENS, NY— APRIL 23

The flight was delayed due to thunderstorms, but nothing could spoil this trip for Trevor. All his friends were stuck in school, but he was free for three glorious weeks.

When the weather cleared and the plane finally took off, they were headed not for Europe but for Georgia.

"Fort Benning's where I went through basic training in 1943," G.G. told the flight attendant.

"Thank you for your service," the woman replied.

"We didn't call it *service* back then," the old soldier said. "We called it *busting Hitler in the chops.*"

"Grandpa," Trevor's dad said patiently, "she's got a lot of other passengers to see to."

"Don't be a wet blanket," G.G. told him.

"We're retracing my great-grandfather's steps through the war," Trevor explained to the flight attendant, "finishing up in the French village he helped liberate. He's getting a medal there."

"Better late than never," G.G. added.

She smiled. "I know you all must be very proud."

When they landed in Atlanta, the airline made the mistake

of offering them an electric cart ride through the sprawling terminal to the baggage claim.

G.G.'s eyes flashed. "I hoofed it across Europe and I can make it around your fool airport."

Dad translated: "He says thanks but no thanks."

They reached the baggage carousel just as their flight number was posted on the electronic board. Trevor's suitcase appeared first, followed a few minutes later by Dad's garment bag. What came next caused a stir among the assembled passengers: a pile of underwear, at least two dozen pairs of socks, a battered shaving kit, and assorted shoes and articles of clothing. Behind this came the remains of G.G.'s duffel bag, broken open in three places where the duct tape had given way.

"Wouldn't you know it?" The old soldier shook his head in disgust. "That thing survived a whole war. But one little domestic flight and kablooey."

"Oh, so it's the airline's fault," Dad said sarcastically. "Silly me, I thought it had something to do with all that duct tape."

His grandfather glared at him. "If there'd been enough duct tape, it wouldn't have happened."

The old man stepped up onto the carousel, placing his feet astride the moving belt, plucking up his belongings as they passed between his long legs.

"Grandpa!" Dad choked.

"I'll help!" Cackling with glee, Trevor leaped onto the conveyor and began scooping up articles of clothing. "Hey, G.G., how come you packed so many socks?"

"I got trench foot after Sainte-Régine," his great-grandfather replied, rescuing a well-worn suit jacket. "I promised myself if I ever went back to France I'd bring plenty of dry socks."

Daniel Firestone lost it completely. "Grandpa! Trevor! Get down from there!"

Finally, security shut down the carousel and the Firestones were able to recover all of G.G.'s property. Dad bought a suitcase from an airport luggage shop, and with much complaining, Jacob Firestone's World War II duffel bag reached the end of its life in a trash can at the car rental center.

"Should we salute it?" Trevor asked as they stood over the mass of canvas and duct tape.

"No need," G.G. told him solemnly. "You can't look back. You've got to keep going."

A few minutes later, the three were in a rented Mazda driving south on Interstate 185 toward Fort Benning, the first stop on Jacob Firestone's journey to Sainte-Régine.

CHAPTER SEVEN

FORT BENNING, GA—OCTOBER 23, 1943

"I can't stand the paratroopers," Jacob panted, sidestepping a white birch tree. "They think they own the world."

Jacob first became a member of Bravo Company at Fort Benning, and many of the men he went to France with started out right there with him, in basic training.

"Never trust a man who spends his time folding silk," added Leland Estrada, gasping at his side on the long run.

Basic training was like gym class times infinity, if you added in guns, grenades, and hand-to-hand combat. Also, gym class ended. This never did. No weekends, no days off, not even any breaks. Everything here was a rush, a hurry—you knew that because there was a drill sergeant every three feet yelling at you to do it faster.

Jacob had already lost sight of the fact that the whole purpose of this was to serve his country. At Fort Benning, there was no time for thinking—only for staying conscious and putting one foot in front of the other at top speed on this twelve-kilometer loop through the woods (timed, of course, carrying rifles and full packs).

It was pure misery. But instead of beating Jacob down, the way it did some of the recruits, it made him stubborn. He was going to get through this because he refused to give the army the satisfaction of defeating him. There were only two ways to come out of basic training—tough or dead. Not dying was the closest he was ever going to get to revenge on the drill instructors.

The instructors worked hard to be hated, and they succeeded beyond their wildest dreams. But they were only third on the enemies list. Number two was Adolf Hitler and the German army. And number one was the paratroopers. Or, as they preferred to be called, the airborne infantry. Big fat hairy deal.

They weren't even paratroopers yet. After basic, they would have to make it through jump school, just like Jacob and the rest of Bravo would go on to infantry training. But even here, where everybody was sort of equal, those future airborne units were considered the crème de la crème.

"What's so bad about paratroopers?" asked Freddie Altman, the third recruit running with them.

"Don't you see them strutting around the post, looking down on the rest of us?" Jacob snorted. "Calling us mud-eaters."

"Just because they get paid an extra fifty bucks a month," Leland put in. "And for what? Jumping out of airplanes. Everybody knows infantry does the real fighting in this army."

At that moment, a group of five airborne recruits loped past them, not even breathing hard.

The lead runner looked back and grinned into Jacob's face. "If you haven't turned up by midnight, we'll send out a search party."

Another kicked Freddie's heel as he jogged by, sending him sprawling in a heap.

The last of the paratroopers, a big Texan named Beau Howell, stopped and helped Freddie up. "Sorry, fellas. I swear we're not all jerks." He sprinted off to join his team.

"Beau's not so terrible," Leland pointed out once the three were moving again.

"He's not a real paratrooper," Jacob explained. "Word around the post is he's only doing it for the extra pay so he can afford to marry his girl back home after the war. He's not a stuck-up silk jockey like the rest of the 'elite.'"

"Well, you have to admit they really are elite," Freddie conceded. "They win everything. Marksmanship, parade, obstacle course, maneuvers, weapons. They even post the best times running the loop. Face it—they're better than us."

For Jacob, those were fighting words. "I'll bet you a month's pay that Bravo beats the airborne at inter-squad next week."

"Then you're going to be a poor man," Leland replied readily, "because I don't know a guy on post who wouldn't take a piece of that action. How are we going to make that happen? Draft Jesse Owens?"

Jacob didn't have the faintest idea. But he had complete confidence that he could work it out. "There's always a way."

The smell of basic training was a tug-of-war between gunpowder, diesel fuel, shoe polish, and sweat. Sweat always won, because every activity had perspiration pouring off the recruits. In 1943, there were almost a hundred thousand of them on the post. It added up to an ocean of sweat.

It was that observation that led Jacob to what he called his "glorious plan to restore honor to the infantry" by knocking the paratroopers down a few pegs. The weapon: salt.

He went into action two days before the inter-squad competitions. He bribed, cajoled, and called in favors with the kitchen staff at the airborne's mess hall to begin oversalting the food. It required a fine hand. The meals had to be salty, but not inedible. That went for the eggs at breakfast, the chipped beef at lunch, and the stew at dinner. Even the coffee was a target, where salty passed for sweet.

"You'll never get away with it," Leland warned. "They're going to notice."

And the paratroopers *did* notice, but in a way that not even Jacob had anticipated. They *liked* it. Instead of being bland and awful, the food was tasty. After weeks of mass-produced military cooking, anything that added flavor was an improvement. The cooks were amazed. The complaints had stopped. Even some actual compliments were coming their way.

"If I didn't know better, I'd swear the cooks were saving the good stuff for them," Freddie commented. "I've got half a mind to sneak into their mess hall just to see what all the fuss is about."

"Don't do it," Jacob warned. "Salt dehydrates you. We've got a twelve-klick race to win tomorrow."

The morning of the competition, the paratroopers' oatmeal

was especially delicious, with heaps of brown sugar covering up the fact that it was 30 percent salt.

When the race began, the airborne jumped out to their usual lead. But as the tough course took its toll, their bodies began to sweat out moisture they didn't have. Within the first few kilometers, their canteens were empty and most of the challenging course still lay ahead.

Running steadily, Jacob and his squad passed the first exhausted paratrooper, doubled over by a tree, clinging to a low branch and sucking air.

"You know the motto of the infantry?" Jacob called as he and his group jogged past. "It's *Follow me!*"

One by one, Jacob ran by every single oversalted airborne recruit. Beau was the last, the iron man. He made it more than eight kilometers in before dehydration, exhaustion, and stomach cramps reduced his progress to a stagger.

Out of compassion and friendship, Bravo left him with a canteen and galloped on to victory.

CHAPTER EIGHT

FORT BENNING, GA—APRIL 24

The satisfaction spilled out of ninety-three-year-old Jacob Firestone as he gestured toward some woods in a distant portion of the sprawling property of Fort Benning. "The finish line was right around there, I think. We busted across it like conquering heroes, let me tell you. They had to send jeeps to pick up most of the paratroopers."

The Firestones had arrived at the post's visitor center in the early afternoon, and were enjoying Jacob's memories of basic training.

Trevor was wide-eyed. "Did you ever get caught?"

G.G. shrugged. "Who was going to turn me in? The mess staff? The civilians would have gotten fired, and the GIs would have been court-martialed along with me. I was safe as houses."

"So the moral of the story is crime pays," Trevor's dad put in disapprovingly. "That's an excellent message for your twelve-year-old great-grandson."

The old soldier glared at him. "That's what you got out of this? The kid knows exactly what the moral is. Tell him, Trev."

"That lots of salt makes crummy food taste okay?" Trevor ventured.

"Ha! That too!" G.G. beamed. "The lesson is you don't let

any high and mighty jerks treat you like a second-class citizen."

"I guess that is a pretty good lesson," Dad admitted.

"What happened to Beau?" Trevor asked. "You said he was a paratrooper. But he was your best friend in the war, right?"

"He washed out of jump school, so they sent him back to Bravo. Fear of heights—who knew? The pay cut didn't hold him back. He married that girl anyway. Nice lady." Jacob's eyes took on a sad, faraway look.

"Beau passed away a few years ago," Dad explained to Trevor.

G.G. made a face. "He didn't pass anything; he died. Why do we have to soft-pedal it? It works that way for everybody. First you're alive and then you're not."

As an alumnus of the infantry and a World War II vet, the old soldier was treated with a lot of respect on the post. They even assigned a jeep and driver to give him and his party a tour of the more than eight hundred square kilometers that made up Fort Benning. G.G. tried to send the man away, saying he didn't need a ride, having run the length and breadth of this place fifty times over. But Dad insisted, and Trevor was grateful. He'd never driven in a real army vehicle before.

Fort Benning had changed a lot since G.G.'s time there, and the old man took it personally. "Those aren't barracks—not *my* barracks anyway. How are you supposed to toughen up soldiers when they live in a five-star hotel?"

The obstacles on the obstacle course weren't high enough; the climbing ropes were too low; the shooting range was manicured like a golf course; the recruits looked like fifth graders who thought they were at Club Med; and the drill instructors barely raised their voices.

"Are you kidding?" Trevor protested. "They're yelling their heads off!"

"That's not yelling," G.G. scoffed. "In my day, if your eardrum wasn't rattling against your brain stem, you couldn't hear what it was they wanted you to do."

Their driver laughed appreciatively. "You're right, sir. Recruits have changed over the years, and the army has had to make a few adjustments. The training is tougher than ever, but there are a few more comforts. Better bunks, more choice in the mess hall—"

"Choice!" the old soldier snorted. "We had a choice—eat or starve. Let me tell you, sometimes starve was the tastier option."

"Maybe it needed salt," Trevor teased.

His great-grandfather snickered. "Shhh! You trying to get me caught after all these years?"

G.G.'s mood improved when they toured the National Infantry Museum. There were exhibits commemorating great battles from the Revolutionary War to modern times. Suddenly, Trevor found himself surrounded by the equipment that had made World War II the largest, most destructive military conflict in human history—tanks, jeeps, parachutes, flamethrowers. He melted into the exhibits, absorbing every detail. Unlike World War I and everything that had come before, World

War II was the first conflict of speed and mobility. Germany was able to conquer the armies of Europe not by outgunning them but by outrunning them. Their strategy of blitzkrieg—lightning war—enabled them to outflank and encircle their enemies. It ushered in the age of mechanized warfare—not just deadlier weapons but faster ones—tanks, half-tracks, mobile artillery, airplanes. And when the Allies landed in Normandy and liberated the continent, they did it with speed of their own, helped along by the greatest buildup of manpower and equipment the world had ever seen.

Trevor tore his eyes from Hermann Goering's captured diamond-encrusted field marshal's baton and regarded his great-grandfather in awe. The Allied victory may have been the single most important historical event of all time, but the infantry museum made one thing clear: World War II wasn't won by giants, but by the courage and deeds of individual soldiers, one at a time. Soldiers just like Private Firestone.

At that moment, G.G. was at the base of a reproduction of the Normandy cliffs. He stood between two life-sized models of soldiers at the foot of the escarpment, looking very much like one of them—which, of course, he had been, so many years ago. The three of them—the old man and the two statues—gazed up to the top of the ridge, where another "soldier" was cresting the rise. G.G. knew what awaited that infantryman as he went over the top, where the wrath of the German defenders would come down on him. Trevor had read books about it, seen movies that depicted it, and played video games that re-created it. But only his great-grandfather had lived it. From the look on his face, he was still living it today.

A video-game designer might be able to re-create this cliff and populate it with soldiers, machine guns, and tanks. But G.G.'s expression—and the experience that had put it there—came from another place entirely.

CHAPTER NINE

ABOARD THE SS *LADY CLAIRE*, MID–ATLANTIC—MARCH 2, 1944

Sardines had it better than this.

The Atlantic crossing to England made Jacob think fondly of basic training at Fort Benning.

They told the 8,900 soldiers crammed aboard that the SS *Lady Claire* had been a luxury ocean liner before it was converted for troop transport. Well, maybe so. But the army had converted the luxury right out of it.

The bunks were stacked five high. Mailboxes got more space than that. If you tried to turn over, you'd brush against the sagging backside of the guy in the bunk sixteen inches above you.

Jacob delivered a sharp knee into the rounded canvas of the berth directly over him. "Hey—quit hogging my sleeping space!"

The lump shifted and Beau's outraged face peered down into Jacob's bunk. "What's the big idea, High School?"

"No wonder you washed out of airborne," Jacob needled. "What parachute could hold up a caboose like yours?"

"One more wisecrack like that," Beau cautioned, "and I'm not going to let you into my war." He swung out a leg and dropped to the deck. "Let's get a head start on the chow line."

"Good idea," Jacob agreed.

Head starts were important aboard the *Lady Claire*. As a cruise ship, she had carried approximately 1,200 passengers. Now she was packed with nearly nine thousand soldiers, which meant there was a line for everything—the heads, the sinks, the showers, the galley. Even deck space to breathe some cold, fresh air was a precious commodity.

At least half the men aboard were from the heartland and had never seen the ocean before, much less traveled on it. Many spent the twelve-day voyage leaning over the rail, violently seasick. Leland Estrada of Omaha was one of them.

"Hey, Leland," Beau called, "if you see a periscope down there, make sure to puke on it!"

Leland turned a green face toward Jacob and Beau. "I'm dying and you're cracking wise. What can a U-boat do to me that's worse than what the army did when they put me on this tub?"

Jacob kept his mouth shut. He didn't like jokes about periscopes. There were hundreds of German submarines prowling the Atlantic, looking to torpedo troop transports before they could unload their soldiers and cargo in England. Having one of them find you was a real possibility. Hundreds of ships had been sunk already, tens of thousands of lives lost. Jacob knew the risks of fighting for his country. But the thought of being blown up at sea like a target in a carnival game—before he could even make his contribution to the war effort—was too awful to think about.

The *Lady Claire* was far from alone on this crossing. She and an even larger troop ship, the *McAllister*, were being escorted by a convoy support group of six navy destroyers, also known as a Hunter-Killer Group. It was a confident, almost brash name, if you didn't think too much about what they were hunting and killing—German U-boats that were equally brash and confident about hunting and killing.

No matter where Jacob looked over the rail, he would see some member of the group around them. Lieutenant McCoy had assured his soldiers that these voyages to England were safer than they'd ever been at any time in the war. It was comforting until you looked out at the black water of the Atlantic, stretching to the horizon in every direction. It was a very large ocean to patrol—especially since the convoy support group had to be right all the time, and the U-boats only had to be right once.

"Come on, Leland," Beau called. "We're going to get some breakfast. That'll make you feel better."

The idea of food turned the Nebraskan's face even greener. "You're a cruel person, you know that?" he harangued, then hung his head over the rail once again.

🚶 🚶 🚶 🚶

Jacob and Beau were waiting in the chow line when the alert sounded. The clatter of trays hitting the deck momentarily drowned out the klaxon. In emergencies, the soldiers were ordered to put on their life jackets, called Mae Wests. Nobody did that. The companionways that led to the overcrowded bunks became instantly impassible. Jacob and Beau headed topside to find a full-fledged naval operation under way.

Barrel-sized depth charges dropped by the dozens from the destroyers. Hundreds of anti-submarine mortars were fired into the sea. It could only mean one thing: Sonar had detected U-boats in the area.

A moment later, the weapons began detonating. Geysers of water shot skyward all around the *Lady Claire*. The ship began to bob and toss from the disturbance.

Jacob focused on a long, sleek shape moving just below the surface of the ocean. At first, it looked almost like a barracuda, but it was too rigid, its path too straight.

"Torpedo!" he exclaimed in horror.

Thousands of pairs of eyes focused on the missile as it cut through the waves, seemingly on a collision course with the *Lady Claire*'s stern. Jacob lost sight of it and braced himself for the devastating impact. He thought of his Mae West, stashed below his bunk, so far out of reach. Was this the careless mistake that would spell the difference between life and death?

Beau grabbed him by the arm. "Can you swim?"

"Not all the way to England!"

The explosion came. But it wasn't nearly as loud or jarring as they expected.

"The *McAllister*!" someone shouted.

A few hundred meters off their stern, orange flame shot from a spot near the bow of the huge troop carrier, right at the waterline. Horrified, Jacob had no idea what to expect next. In newsreel footage, he had seen ships sink out of sight in what seemed to be mere minutes. But the *McAllister* just wallowed there as sailors and soldiers ran frantically about the deck, scrambling into life jackets.

He had never felt more powerless. Here he was, part of a force of nearly nine thousand soldiers. Yet there was nothing he could do to help the crippled *McAllister* or to take part in the battle against the enemy submarine that still menaced the convoy.

And then, just as suddenly, the fighting ceased. The depth charges and mortars stopped. The destroyers began to move to the aid of the *McAllister*.

Jacob found himself shaking like a leaf. "How come we've stopped shooting? The U-boat could still be down there!"

Beau shook his head. "I don't think so, High School. Take a look."

Off to starboard, pieces of black metal debris were bobbing to the surface amid a spreading oil slick.

Jacob was still panicked. "Okay, so we got one, but there could be others, right? The Germans made more than one submarine!"

"We've got sonar," Beau reminded him. "If there were more of them, we'd know. This isn't a battle anymore. It's a rescue operation. Let's see if we can volunteer to help get those poor devils off the *McAllister*."

The waves continued to churn up pieces of U-boat, oil-stained and burned. There was food from the galley and a few life jackets. *They didn't have time to get to them*, Jacob thought to himself. Not once before had he considered the submarine a vehicle filled with human beings rather than a mechanical killing machine.

There was a bubble of air and a new piece of debris broke the surface. It was the remains of a German sailor, blown up, or drowned, or maybe both.

It was the first dead body Jacob Firestone had ever seen.

CHAPTER TEN

LONDON, ENGLAND—APRIL 26

London was one of the world's great cities, filled with cultural treasures like Buckingham Palace, Big Ben, Kew Gardens, Shakespeare's Globe Theatre, and the Tower of London, where the Crown Jewels were on display.

Trevor didn't want to see any of it.

"That stuff's too boring," he argued. "Nobody wants to stand in line to look at old paintings and furniture. London was ground zero during the Battle of Britain. There were constant air raids and attacks with buzz bombs and V-2 rockets. People put up blackout curtains so the German pilots would have nothing to aim at because the city was dark. Over thirty thousand people died in the bombing. Almost ninety thousand were injured. Two million homes were destroyed. *That's* what I want to see."

"I hate to break it to you," his father said dryly, "but it was seventy-five years ago. There aren't any piles of rubble, Trevor. They built it all back up again."

Trevor reddened. "I know *that*. But you can still go down to the Tube stations Londoners used as bomb shelters during the air raids. And don't forget Saint Paul's Cathedral—people actually climbed up onto the dome to make sure bombs didn't fall on it. They were batting them away with brooms—bombs that could have gone off in their faces. Even the royal family helped out—Queen Elizabeth was an ambulance driver during her princess days. You hear a lot about individual heroes, but in the Battle of Britain, a whole country rose up and refused to be defeated."

Dad relented. "Fine. We'll take the rubble tour. This whole trip is about the war. We might as well do wartime London."

There turned out to be plenty to explore. They started at the Imperial War Museum, then toured the battleship HMS *Belfast*, which was moored at the Queen's Walk. They also visited the Churchill War Rooms, where Trevor could almost feel the presence of the famous prime minister and the weight of the momentous decisions that had been made there.

G.G. tried to find a pub he'd once visited on a weekend pass, but when Trevor looked the location up on his phone, it was a Starbucks now.

"You can't go home again," the old man put in wanly.

The next morning, the Firestones were on a train, heading south for Portsmouth, which was where Bravo Company had sailed for France.

The three had been riding for about an hour and a half when G.G. suddenly leaped to his feet.

"Grandpa!" Trevor's dad was alarmed. "What's wrong?"

The old man began pulling luggage down from the

overhead rack. "Didn't you hear the announcement? Petersfield! I trained there!"

Trevor was instantly on his feet, helping his great-grandfather gather their belongings as the train began to slow.

Dad was flustered. "But our tickets are to Portsmouth! Our hotel reservations—"

"We'll just have to be late," G.G. decided. "We can't miss this. I was in a sausage here for three months."

Trevor was bug-eyed. "A sausage?"

"It's what the Brits called them," the old man explained briskly, hustling the three of them up the aisle, baggage and all. "The whole invasion force—they had us in camps across the south of England. The muck-a-mucks in charge of the war drew circles all over the map, and somebody thought they looked like sausages."

The train came to a halt, and a conductor helped the Firestones unload their belongings onto the platform. Then the doors slid shut and the train chugged away, stranding them in a small village with a high street of neat shops.

Dad sighed. "Aw, Grandpa, why did we have to do this? Now we're nowhere."

"We're not nowhere," Trevor amended. "We're in the *sausage*."

G.G. ambled over to the single taxicab waiting on the street. After a long conversation with many hand gestures, the driver came out to load their luggage into the car.

They drove off. Within a few minutes, they had left Petersfield, and the Hampshire countryside surrounded them.

Aside from the taxi's engine, the only sound was the soft bleating of countless sheep from the fields on both sides of the road.

"They loaded us up on trucks and took us to the camp," G.G. recalled. "And you know what was all around us? Sheep, baaing their heads off."

"How far to the sausage?" Trevor asked.

"Not too much farther," the old soldier replied. "We should be coming up on it soon."

Trevor craned his neck, anxious for a first glimpse of the place that had served as Jacob Firestone's jumping-off point to World War II.

CHAPTER ELEVEN

PETERSFIELD, ENGLAND—APRIL 29, 1944

Private Freddie Altman pushed up the sleeve of his uniform jacket and consulted his watch. "How much farther away is this? If the lieutenant catches us off post, it's latrine duty for the rest of the war."

"Just till the invasion," Beau amended. "Scrubbing toilets is fine until they need us for something more important—like getting shot."

"It's just past these trees," Jacob insisted.

They pushed through some heavy underbrush and stepped out through the last of the forest. Stretched before them was a jaw-dropping sight. Tanks, half-tracks, trucks, and jeeps were parked in never-ending rows, so close that you couldn't see the ground between them. Artillery cannons and anti-aircraft guns—hundreds of acres of them—were arranged beyond that.

"I've never seen anything like this before," Leland commented in awe. "Not even at Benning."

"This isn't for any training exercise," Beau explained. "This is for the real thing. This is our present for Hitler."

"How are we going to get it across the channel?" Freddie asked.

"Good thing you're not a general," Jacob observed. "Didn't you see all those ships in the exercise? That's just a fraction of what we've got."

The previous week, the entire corps had participated in an exercise code-named Tiger—a simulated invasion on the English coast. The fleet had been enormous.

Leland lowered his voice. "Do you think what they're saying is true?"

The word was spreading through the tightly packed "sausages" of southern England that German torpedo boats had infiltrated the fleet during the night and attacked the larger ships, sinking at least two. Soldiers were notorious for blowing rumors out of proportion, but there were stories circulating that as many as a thousand men had gone missing and probably drowned. Lieutenant McCoy and Captain Marone were keeping a tight lid on any information about what had happened.

Freddie was frustrated. "How come the officers won't tell us the truth?"

"Bad news is bad for morale," Beau replied. "If we can't stage an exercise in our own territory without losing people, how are we supposed to invade France?"

"Are you telling me the army cares about my morale?" Jacob indicated the vast array of military firepower before them. "You know how much of this we're going to get? A shovel. That's all I've done since coming to England—dig foxholes. If I ever come face-to-face with Hitler, I'm going to have to beat him over the head with my shovel."

"'*Your rifle may win the war, but your shovel will save your life,*'" the others chorused, quoting Lieutenant McCoy, who was very big on foxhole digging.

"I didn't come halfway around the world to be a ditch-digger," Jacob complained. "I'm here to fight."

Freddie checked his watch again. "Fellas, we've got to *go*. If we're not in the hut for bed check, they'll have the MPs out looking for us. McCoy's already nuts about GIs prowling the pubs and beefing with the locals."

"Don't worry," Beau promised. "I know a shortcut back."

The four soldiers began making their way through the woods, moving rapidly despite the heavy underbrush. Jacob had to give the army credit for that—months of infantry training had made them comfortable traversing all kinds of terrain. But after twenty minutes of hiking, jogging, and jumping fences, even Beau had to admit they were lost. Dusk was already upon them, which meant that they would soon be even more lost. In the south of England, wartime rules demanded full blackout—no lights at all.

A long, low snort sounded uncomfortably close by, followed by the stamping of large hoofs. Red eyes glared at them through the gloom.

"Run!" This from Beau, the Texan, who understood exactly what they were up against.

A Hereford bull exploded out of the growing darkness. By the time the Americans could all make it out, the huge animal was nearly upon them, head down, horns poised.

Jacob, Beau, and Leland scattered, but Freddie stood his

ground. He pulled out his sidearm, prepared to do battle.

"Are you nuts?" Jacob practically shrieked. He spun on a dime and hurled himself, horizontal to the ground, at Freddie. He hit the soldier right at the knees, sending the two of them sprawling. When the bull thundered by, it shook the earth and moved the air. It was that close.

Before the bull could turn around to make another charge at them, Jacob hauled Freddie upright, dragged him to the fence, and heaved the two of them through the rails and into the next pasture.

"You crazy idiot!" Jacob ranted. "That thing would have skewered you like a shish kebab!"

"I would have taken him down," Freddie insisted.

"You think one little bullet would have stopped a monster like that?" Beau panted. "He's a thousand pounds if he's an ounce. His momentum alone would have squashed you like a bug."

"And the lieutenant warned us not to antagonize the locals," added Leland. "We're supposed to act like guests in England. What kind of guest shoots a farmer's bull?"

"I'll bet the cows wouldn't have been too thrilled about it either," Jacob added.

It broke the mood. The four chuckled as they made their way back to camp.

"That was pretty impressive, High School," Beau commented. "Throwing yourself in front of a charging bull. I think you're destined to be a hero. I'm going to stick close to you when we get to France. The next life you save could be mine."

The Texan was joking as usual, but it made Jacob think. At this point, the soldiers of Bravo Company were about as hardened and well trained as it was possible to be. The one thing they could not know was how they would react to the life-and-death conditions of the battlefield. Had he received his first clue? Seeing Freddie in the bull's path, Jacob had thrown himself into danger without a moment's hesitation.

Maybe he really *was* destined to be a hero. Either that, or the fool who does something stupid and gets everybody killed.

Blundering through the near-total darkness, they got back to their Nissen hut late for bed check, earning themselves a face-to-face with Lieutenant McCoy.

"We've got live fire exercises at 0800 tomorrow, and you four have just volunteered to take the forward positions."

In the morning, Bravo Company was loaded onto trucks and brought to some hilly country east of camp. To simulate real battle conditions, no one was told the exact nature of the exercise. Their only instructions were to dig in and await developments.

"Figures," Jacob mumbled as his shovel bit through the hard ground of the slope. "Disciplinary action or no, we're always digging foxholes."

"Better than latrine duty," called Leland from the position to his left.

"Maybe," Jacob shot back grudgingly.

"Make them deep like your life depends on it!" McCoy hollered. "Because it does!"

As Jacob dug, perspiration poured from underneath his helmet and into his stinging eyes, forming a clammy, uncomfortable layer of moisture beneath his wool jacket. His uniform stuck to him. No weather conditions, even at the North Pole, could ever be cold enough to avoid sweat while digging a foxhole. It was an infantry regulation: You were required to be covered in sweat at all times or you weren't doing it right. It was the only thing he regretted about his decision to join the army.

Exhausted, he climbed into the hole, thinking yearningly of his parents' house in Connecticut and the dry clothes in his closet.

"Hey, High School," Beau hissed. "Not deep enough! Your head's sticking out!"

"Let McCoy court-martial me," he stage-whispered in reply. "I can't face one more shovelful."

At that moment a roaring sound swelled on the other side of the hill. A moment later seven big Sherman tanks crested the rise, firing live ammunition. Jacob could feel the air currents created by one of the shells passing maybe six inches over his helmet.

He bent his knees in an attempt to collapse into his hole, but the opening was too narrow for him to get low. The tanks continued to fire as they advanced on the dug-in soldiers.

That was when he saw it—one of the Shermans was coming directly at him.

"Hey! Veer off! Veer off!"

It was impossible for the tank crew to hear him over the booming of the guns and the rumble of the engines.

The tank was less than ten feet away, its left tread poised to pass directly over the foxhole. There was no time to climb out and run for it. Panic-stricken, Jacob came to a desperate decision. The hole would just have to make room for him.

He pressed his knees and face against the earthen wall and twisted his body, like he was a human drill bit.

The clatter of the Sherman passing overhead blotted out everything but noise and pressure. For several agonizing seconds, he actually felt the tread making contact with the top of his helmet.

Then it passed. Daylight returned and he was still alive.

Jacob remained unmoving in his foxhole, barely allowing himself to breathe, even when the roar of the Sherman faded and McCoy pronounced the exercise a success.

Finally, Beau hauled the still-trembling Jacob out of the ground.

"Jeez, High School—you know you got tank tracks on your helmet?"

Jacob never complained about digging foxholes again.

CHAPTER TWELVE

CROSSING THE ENGLISH CHANNEL— APRIL 28

The journey across the English Channel from Portsmouth, UK, to Cherbourg, France, was the coldest boat ride Trevor had ever experienced. The temperature wasn't much below sixty degrees, and it never actually rained. But there was a constant mist driven by strong winds. The *Normandie Express*—a huge catamaran ferry—was topped by a vast circular sundeck. The only thing missing was sun. Ten minutes on deck, exposed to the elements, left you drenched and half-frozen.

No wonder G.G. was wearing a heavy wool peacoat. "I told you two idiots to bring something warm," he informed his grandson and great-grandson with a superior smirk. "The Channel has a climate all its own."

Trevor hugged his light jacket to his sides and tried to shrink into the collar. "How do the people who live here stand such awful weather?"

"Awful?" the old soldier crowed. "This is the good weather. When it's awful, you've got gale-force winds and fog so thick you need radar to find your way to the latrine."

Dad stood a short distance away, holding up his phone in

search of a signal. "Isn't this ferry supposed to have Wi-Fi? I can't pick up the network."

"It's probably the weather," G.G. said, inhaling a lungful of cold, damp air as if he were enjoying a garden of hyacinths. "Back in the war, it got so nasty that Eisenhower had to postpone the whole invasion. Picture that—more than one hundred fifty thousand soldiers, sailors, and airmen getting told 'Sorry, we'll try again tomorrow.'"

"I read about that," Trevor confirmed. "D-Day was originally supposed to be June fifth, right?"

His great-grandfather nodded. "Ike pushed back the entire operation thanks to a forty-knot wind and a cloud cover like pea soup. It wasn't so much about the fleet—what's a little extra seasickness from a bunch of poor saps who've been barfing nonstop since England? But the planes wouldn't be able to see where they were dropping their paratroopers and gliders. And forget about air support."

"And the next day it cleared up?" Trevor queried.

"Dream on. The next day it improved to just bad." The old man gestured around them on the ferry. "Like this. If we'd held out for good weather, we'd still be waiting."

"At least you got the extra day, though," Trevor commented. "You know, to get psyched up for battle."

"Are you kidding? By that point, I'd spent almost a whole year of my life preparing for one thing—*this*, the invasion of Europe. Sure, I was scared about what would happen. But mostly, I wanted to get it over with. It had to be done and we were the ones who had to do it. I was packed onto a troop carrier—one of thousands of ships. We were going—and then we were turning around. For days, we'd been writing our wills and saying our prayers, sending letters home that might be the last time our families would ever hear from us. Guys were rubbing rabbits' feet and having whole conversations with four-leaf clovers. My buddy Beau was jumping into every card game that would have him, determined to gamble away all his money so he could hit the beaches flat broke, with nothing to lose. We were barely human beings at that point. We were trained killers, half-nuts with tension, half-dead with seasickness. The last thing we needed was twenty-four more hours to stew in it."

Dad was shaking his phone as if he believed that motion might attract the ferry's Wi-Fi. Exasperated, Trevor took the device from him, fiddled with it for a few moments, and handed it back.

"Here you go. You had the password wrong. It's *Normandie* with an *i-e*—the French spelling."

"Thanks," his father acknowledged a little sheepishly.

The crossing, which had taken all night for the D-Day fleet, was only a three-hour journey for the speedy *Normandie Express*. Two hours in, the coast of France began to appear on the misty horizon.

Trevor's voice suddenly became husky with excitement. "Is that where the invasion happened?"

G.G. shook his head. "That's the Cotentin Peninsula. The landing sites were off to the left. The side of that land strip—that's Utah Beach. Then comes Omaha, where I landed. The

British and Canadian beaches—Sword, Juno, and Gold—are farther off."

The code names seemed to echo in Trevor's head: Sword, Juno, Gold, Omaha, Utah. The five Normandy landing spots that signified the beginning of the end for Hitler's Third Reich. How many times had Trevor read those words in books and on the Internet, heard them in movies and video games? Only now, they were real. He was *here*—or at least almost here. An hour offshore from the famous places, where so many heroes had been forged under fire, where so many lives had tragically come to an end.

Now finally connected to Wi-Fi, Daniel was at the rail, checking the Sainte-Régine Facebook page. There were the usual comments expressing excitement about the upcoming celebration. Several old-timers had posted pictures of the village before the war, and during its rebuilding afterward. Residents who now lived in Paris and other cities were planning on coming home for the festivities. There was a little griping about the availability of hotels in the area. Some of the locals were renting out rooms to visitors. And—

What he saw next chilled him even more than the wind off the water.

The post was from La Vérité, like some of the ones he'd seen before. The group had been becoming increasingly angry with the town for inviting Jacob Firestone to be honored at the ceremony. He was not a hero, they insisted, and the group had information that would show that he'd been responsible for the deaths of many Frenchmen.

All those things had been said before, but in this most recent message, La Vérité finished with:

> At this very moment, Jacob Firestone is on his way to the shores of
> our beloved France. If we celebrate him in Sainte-Régine, it will be
> a stain on our village and an insult to our honored dead.

Daniel blinked. *On his way to the shores of our beloved France.* How could they know that? Who were these people? Were they spying on the Firestones? He glanced around the deck, as if expecting to see enemies in trench coats, watching them through narrowed eyes behind sunglasses.

He pulled himself up short, feeling a little foolish. There were no enemies on the boat—and certainly no sunglasses in this dark overcast.

Still, there were other ways to spy these days. Airline tickets, hotel reservations, rental cars—they were all made electronically. Which meant the Firestones' travel plans were knowable to anyone with computer skills.

The question was, what should they do about it? Another hour would put them in France. It would be crazy to turn back now. Over what? Facebook posts? Grandpa would never accept that. And Trevor would be even worse.

On the other hand, these were threats—almost. For sure, La Vérité was accusing Grandpa of terrible things. And Grandpa hadn't exactly denied them—he'd just muttered something about the past catching up with him. What was that supposed to mean? Did he really have blood on his hands? Well, why wouldn't he? He was an active-duty soldier in the middle of a giant shooting war.

Would Grandpa be safe in Sainte-Régine? Would any of them be?

On the phone, the screen refreshed and La Vérité's message disappeared. Daniel felt a little better. That meant that somebody in Sainte-Régine was monitoring the page and deleting the offending posts. At least someone in the village was on Grandpa's side. He frowned. It also meant that there had probably been even more posts—ones that had been taken down before he'd had a chance to read them and be warned.

He looked across the deck to where his grandfather and son stood side by side at the rail. The old man was pointing ashore while Trevor watched in rapt attention. Daniel Firestone knew then that he could never put an end to this trip. Besides, La Vérité was probably nothing more than some Internet troll who didn't like Americans very much. It didn't make sense to let someone like that spoil the trip of a lifetime.

🚶 🚶 🚶 🚶

Soon, the city of Cherbourg loomed up ahead. The *Normandie Express* pulled into a slip and the passengers and crew prepared to disembark.

The wharf bustled with baggage handlers, taxi drivers, and other people greeting the new arrivals. It was a busy place, so no one paid much attention to a motorcycle leaning against a pylon at the far end of the dock. Beside it stood two leather-clad teenagers—a seventeen-year-old boy and his cousin, a thirteen-year-old girl.

They were acting very casual, but both kept sharp eyes on the stream of passengers coming down the gangway.

The girl held two photographs in her hand. One was a black-and-white picture of a young American wearing the uniform of the United States Infantry: Private Jacob Firestone. The second was color: the old soldier as he appeared today.

Five minutes later, the very same man stepped onto French soil for the first time in seventy-five years.

CHAPTER THIRTEEN

OFF THE COAST OF NORMANDY, FRANCE—JUNE 6, 1944

Five thousand ships—the largest fleet ever assembled.

Across the darkened Channel they sailed, a vast column many miles across. It reminded Jacob of New York City, only instead of a skyline of buildings, this was a landscape of the conning towers of battleships, destroyers, and troop transports. It almost looked like you could cross all the way to France without getting your feet wet, just by jumping from boat to boat to boat.

Watching from his Haskell-class Attack Transport Ship, Jacob had never been so physically uncomfortable. He was seasick from the rough crossing, exhausted from tension and lack of sleep, weighed down by equipment, and jam-packed on the deck among the rest of Bravo Company and all the other companies in the battalion, and the other battalions in the regiment. And yet, in the strongest sense since his arrival at Fort Benning, he felt the patriotic spirit that had drawn him to the recruitment center in the first place. Hitler's Germany was threatening the world, and at long last, the world had an answer: this vast armada.

And he was a part of it.

As the Normandy coast appeared, a dark strip in the gray predawn, an odd quiet descended on the troops around Jacob. It was their first glimpse of the objective they had been training for these many months. The urge to get there had been all-consuming. But now that it was before them, they recognized it as the place where many of their young lives would end. That was not merely a possibility; it was a cold, hard fact.

As they drew closer, a phalanx of minesweepers took the lead. Spaced out across the entire invasion zone, these small boats employed broad underwater nets to clear the shipping lanes of hundreds of mines laid by the Nazi defenders. There were muffled explosions and geysers of water shooting up from the surface. As the sweepers advanced, they floated marker buoys to show the safe routes to shore.

Behind them, the large battleships took their positions. Their big guns could pound targets miles away, along the beaches, the bluffs, and even inland. It was their job to soften up the defenders for the invading force.

Next came the multitude of troop ships, each one a hive of activity. Winches whirred as thousands of attack boats were filled with soldiers and lowered into the water. Jacob had very little respect for military discipline, but he had to admit that it was coming in handy now. His Attack Transport Ship was utter chaos—more than a thousand soldiers all running in different directions while officers brayed instructions at them. Yet their months of training brought everybody where they were supposed to be with the equipment they were supposed to have.

With the rest of Bravo Company's Third Platoon, Jacob

climbed into the thirty-six-man LCVP—Landing Craft, Vehicle, Personnel, aka a Higgins boat—and settled himself behind the drop gate that would become the off-ramp when they reached the beach.

A hand grabbed him by the collar and dragged him aft. Beau. "You don't want to be the first guy off, High School. Your peach-fuzz cheeks are too fat a target!"

Jacob decided this was pretty good advice. He pressed himself in beside Leland and Freddie. Peering over the gunwale, he could see the other boats tossing in the waves like bouncing Ping-Pong balls. The LCVP was designed to go right up to the beach, so it had a flat bottom—which meant it rode like a bucking bronco on the breakers.

Leland—who had the worst seasickness problems in Bravo Company and possibly the entire Allied Expeditionary Force—was greener than ever. "I'm not going to make it," he said to no one in particular. "I won't even be able to blame it on Hitler."

Last onto the boat was Lieutenant McCoy. He did a quick head count and shouted, "Lower away!"

The mechanism rattled and squeaked as the LCVP began to descend.

Here goes nothing, Jacob thought to himself.

The boat dropped about eight feet then suddenly stalled, swinging on the ropes as the jammed winch jerked to a halt. The smell hit them a moment later—the overpowering stench of raw sewage.

Beau pointed. "We're right below the discharge vent from the heads!"

"Lieutenant, what should we do?" Freddie pleaded.

It was the first time anyone had seen Lieutenant McCoy at a loss for words. Finally, the officer came up with a solution to the problem: "Keep your helmets on, men!"

And there, confronted by the greatest danger he would ever face in a very long lifetime, seventeen-year-old Jacob Firestone got the giggles. At that moment, miles up the coast, the Royal Navy began heavy bombardment of the British and Canadian invasion beaches. It was just after five thirty a.m., with H hour less than sixty minutes away. But, huddled beneath his helmet, Jacob laughed all through it.

"That's some sense of humor you got there, High School," Beau rumbled.

Even after the winch was freed and the LCVP hit the water, Jacob was still cackling. Part of him wondered if the laughter was the only thing keeping him from panicking as their boat began to move toward Omaha Beach and what was sure to be a deadly battle.

Three minutes tossing in the waves wiped any remaining smile off his face. Seasickness was no longer just Leland's problem. Everyone suffered, including Lieutenant McCoy. The struggle to find room at the gunwales became a wrestling match among soldiers who needed to save their energy for what lay ahead.

The sea was so rough that each oncoming wave crashed over the boat, dousing them all with icy water. It helped wash away the vomit and what was left of the raw sewage that had been dumped on them by the ship. In no time, Jacob's thick woolen uniform was so sodden and heavy that the simple act of shifting his position in the boat took all his strength. Between that and his life preserver, pack, rifle, trenching tool, gas mask, first aid kit, knife, grenades, explosives, ammunition, field rations, and canteen, he questioned whether or not he'd even be able to move when they reached the beach.

They were still more than a kilometer offshore when the American fleet opened fire. They could feel the shells screaming overhead. On the bluffs and farther inland, columns of smoke, fire, and debris rose up to color the sky. A moment later, returning fire came from the German batteries onshore.

For most of the Americans, it was the first proof positive that their enemy even existed. Someone was shooting back. In a strange way, their war only started in that instant.

"Keep your heads below the gunwales!" McCoy bellowed.

That was bad news for the seasick men in the Higgins boat. Now they had nowhere to throw up except onto themselves and each other. Luckily, the surging waves continued to wash them clean.

Yet for all the fire that was being exchanged, nothing coming from the shore seemed to be aimed at the landing boats. Didn't the Germans see them? Jacob risked a glance over the side. Their LCVP was one of hundreds that dotted the sea off Normandy. Among them were dozens of larger landing craft, capable of carrying not just soldiers and equipment but tanks and artillery.

"Lieutenant!" Freddie called suddenly. "Are we sinking?"

Jacob looked down. Racked by nausea and stressed beyond

straining, none of the platoon had noticed that they were crouched knee-deep in seawater.

"Ignore it!" McCoy barked. "The boat's unsinkable!"

"That's what they said about the *Titanic*!" Leland wailed.

The lieutenant was adamant. "If the army says it won't sink, then it won't sink!"

In the stern of the LCVP, the radio rang with chatter from the other craft. Over the babble, a terrified voice cried, "We're sinking!"

The men of Bravo Company's Third Platoon pulled off their helmets and began bailing. After a moment's hesitation, their lieutenant joined them.

They were in the line of assault craft, less than two hundred meters from shore, when it happened. A control boat directly ahead of them blew into pieces.

"Mine!" McCoy bellowed, ducking as they were showered with debris.

Jacob stared at the patch of turbulent water where the boat had been seconds before, searching for survivors to drag onto the LCVP. There weren't any. It had been that fast—and that deadly.

To his left, too close for comfort, a large LST—Landing Ship, Tank—opened its gate to deploy its cargo of amphibious tanks. But as the ramp came down, it triggered a booby-trapped underwater obstacle. Jacob could feel the hot wind of the blast on his face, and the roar left him momentarily deafened. A Sherman, its billowing float screen ablaze, lifted twenty feet in the air and hit the water right next to Jacob's Higgins boat, nearly swamping it. If he'd reached out a hand, he would have grazed the cannon on the way down.

"Stop! Stop!" Jacob hollered. "There are wounded in the water!"

"We're not a rescue ship, High School," Beau reminded him grimly. "We only go in one direction." He pointed toward the beach, less than fifty meters away.

A new noise joined the roar of the boats and the booming of artillery—the rapid-fire clang of machine-gun bullets ricocheting off the raised steel ramps that formed the bow of the LCVP. Helmets could be used as bailing buckets no longer. The men of Third Platoon ducked their heads and made themselves extremely small. The time they'd be able to shrink from danger was almost over, but they intended to cling to it as long as they could.

The Higgins boat scraped bottom. H hour. The ramp opened and slapped down into hip-deep water. As Jacob scrambled upright, he saw a platoon charge out of a boat not ten meters away. Machine-gun fire ripped through them, striking down at least half of the soldiers in the blink of an eye.

We have no chance, he thought to himself. *How could anybody ask us to try this?*

He hit the ramp running—high-stepping, knees pumping through the breakers. For several seconds he forgot his training, his orders, and even the fact that there were other people with him. Gunfire rang in his ears—it was everywhere. A bullet plucked at his sleeve, and by instinct he dropped, genuinely amazed to find himself underwater. Choking, he bounced up, praying his rifle would still fire. But fire at what? His fevered mind raced. There was nothing to shoot at. The Germans were at the top of the bluff in pillboxes and machine-gun nests, raining bullets down onto the invaders. Already the shallow water was littered with casualties, some wounded, many dead—and they hadn't even reached dry land yet. Cries of *"Medic!"* rang out amid the chaos.

Jacob charged ashore with the men of the first wave and flattened himself to the rocky beach. Beau was by his side, burrowing like a sand crab, as if trying to bury himself. Jacob couldn't see Freddie, but he could hear Leland cursing somewhere behind him. Incredibly, the guy actually sounded a little better, now that he was on solid ground and not seasick anymore.

Bullets sprayed over their heads, but for the moment, couldn't reach them. The beach sloped upward to a seawall a few meters ahead, which provided some shelter from the incoming fire.

Jacob risked a glance over his shoulder. Where were the tanks and artillery pieces? Where were the engineers to clear the way through the mines and obstacles? As he watched in horror, an amphibious tank drove off one of the LSTs and plunged into the sea, disappearing forever.

Beau saw it too. "The plan's a bust!" he howled. "And we're left holding the bag!"

It was true. After all the training and preparation, nothing was happening the way Captain Marone had described in endless briefings. The air-and-sea bombardment had not hindered the enemy's coastal defenses. The boats had run aground on

sandbars far short of the water's edge, forcing the landing par-
ties to slog ashore through deep water, sitting ducks for the
snipers who awaited them. The heavy weapons, armor, and
vehicles were ending up at the bottom of the sea, where they
couldn't support anybody, not even themselves.

Worst of all, the men of the first wave lay wounded or dead
in the surf, or hemmed in on a few meters of beach behind the
seawall. The unit's objectives rattled around in Jacob's head,
words like *Fox White*—their designated landing position. Was
this it? Were they lost? For sure, nothing in this awful and chaotic place resembled the charts and maps they'd been shown.
And with so many of their people suddenly and tragically out
of the picture, did it even matter?

Jacob inched up to the seawall and peered over with one eye.

Beau appeared at his side. "What do you see?"

"Machine-gun nest. Dead ahead, halfway up the bluff.
That's what's got us pinned down."

Both men examined their options. The situation didn't
look promising. Between their position and the base of the
bluff lay two hundred meters of completely open beach. Anyone
trying to cross that gap would be chopped to pieces.

Leland crawled up behind them. "What do we do?"

Beau shrugged. "Do I look like a general to you? How
many stars on this helmet?"

"Where's the lieutenant?" Jacob asked.

"Hit," Leland reported grimly. "Medic's wrapping up his arm."

"Great," said Beau. "The high school kid's in charge."

Jacob looked back toward the armada in the vain hope that

help was on the way. All up and down the beach, troops were landing every minute, coming under the same withering fire. No officer to take command. No miraculous piece of equipment to turn the tide.

Then it happened. A few hundred meters to their right, a Sherman tank roared out of the water and onto the beach, dripping like a wet dog. Why this one tank had survived after so many had foundered, no one knew. It was here, and that was enough.

Bullets bounced off its armor as it roared over the seawall and made a run for the base of the bluff. It picked up speed, firing at the machine-gun nest. The shell ripped into the escarpment just below the German gunners.

"Higher!" Beau bellowed.

Almost as if the tank crew had heard him, the cannon began to crank upward, adjusting its aim.

As the tank moved forward, the swiveling gun made contact with a trip wire attached to a tall obstacle. A dark object swung into the side of the Sherman—an anti-tank mine.

Before Jacob's horrified eyes, the Sherman disappeared in an enormous fireball. There was no chance any of the crew could have survived. A plume of thick black smoke blew diagonally across the sand, directly into Jacob's face. For an instant, Omaha Beach disappeared.

Jacob choked once, then realized what he was looking at. Cover. If he couldn't see the German gunners, they couldn't see him.

"Let's go!" He was up and over the seawall, sprinting through the black smoke.

He heard Beau's voice—"High School, are you crazy?"— followed by an even more terrifying sound: machine-gun fire. Bullets ripped into the sand, perilously close by. But as long as he stayed in the plume of smoke, he knew the gunners couldn't draw a bead on him.

As he ran, he pulled a grenade from his belt. He knew the burning tank was about twenty-five meters from the base of the bluff, but he'd have to leave the cover of the smoke to have any chance of an accurate throw. At that moment, he'd be completely exposed to the guns. If he didn't destroy them, they would most definitely destroy him.

He could see the flames of the Sherman right in front of him, even feel the heat. He pulled the pin as he ran, counted five more strides, and burst into the open.

He reared back his arm even before his eyes zeroed in on the nest. There it was, almost exactly where he'd expected it to be. Breathing a silent prayer that he was more accurate than he'd been when the coach had cut him from JV baseball, he let fly and hit the dirt.

He heard the German gun burst to life, felt the first few rounds pass over his flattened body. The next sound was the explosion of the grenade. The gun fell silent.

Beau galloped up behind him, grabbed him by the collar, and dragged him the rest of the way to the foot of the bluff. Spent and dazed, Jacob tried to spot the nest, but he couldn't find it anymore. At last he spied it, the sandbags blown apart, the weapon disabled.

"The gunners—" he managed.

"You got 'em, High School!" Beau shouted. "You're one crazy, stupid hero!"

Troops streamed across the beach, following Jacob's path through the plume of smoke, Leland in the lead. Another figure ducked out from the shelter of a large hedgehog—a beach obstacle that resembled a gigantic piece from a game of jacks.

"Freddie!" The sight of him brought Jacob back to his feet. He'd been worried that his friend might have been one of the hundreds of crumpled uniforms that dotted the beach like collapsed scarecrows.

Freddie started toward them, waving madly. "We made it! We—"

Freddie never saw the mine, never knew what hit him. Dozens had passed over that very spot. But Freddie's boot came down in the wrong place, and in one violent flash of gunpowder and shrapnel, his war was over.

Jacob, Beau, and Leland could only huddle together and stare as the madness of Omaha Beach raged all around them. It had been that quick, that sudden. An instant ago, they had been a foursome.

Now they were just three.

CHAPTER FOURTEEN

NORMANDY, FRANCE—APRIL 29

"No-o-o-o!" Trevor cried out in shock. "Not Freddie! Freddie can't die!"

G.G. raised both bushy eyebrows. "He could and he did. I'll show you exactly where it happened."

The Firestones waited with about forty fellow tourists aboard the *Fleur de Lys*. The excursion boat was a reconditioned landing craft used on D-Day—not a Higgins boat, but a bigger LCIL, which stood for Landing Craft, Infantry, Large. There were plenty of luxury boat rides to ferry visitors to Normandy's five invasion beaches, but the old soldier had insisted on this one. Only the *Fleur de Lys* could land people virtually the way he and the troops had landed more than seventy-five years before.

"You talked about Freddie a million times, but you never said he *died*," Trevor protested.

"I never said he *didn't* die, did I?" G.G. challenged.

"Well, no, but—"

"Trevor," Dad put in quietly, "maybe Grandpa left out certain details because he felt you weren't mature enough to hear them. War isn't like the video games, you know."

"Are you kidding?" Trevor defended himself. "It's exactly like video games. And, yes, Dad, I get the difference that when you die in real war, you stay dead. I know that. I just didn't know it happened to Freddie, that's all."

"It happened to too many of us that day," G.G. said grimly. "Those tanks that sank before ever firing a shot—they weren't just soulless machines. They had crews in them. Think those poor fools had a chance to get out?"

Everyone was jostled as the LCIL ran gently aground. An announcement sounded in several languages that the gate was about to lower. There was a stir of excitement.

Trevor closed his eyes and imagined what it must have been like on G.G.'s Higgins boat—the spray of the surf, the clang of bullets on the iron gate, the fear of knowing that your life could end at any second.

The gate rattled down and there was Omaha Beach.

"It's peaceful," Trevor said in a hushed voice.

"Yeah, sure," the old man agreed. "Today."

The shoreline lay before them, looking nothing like its storied past. A handful of people strolled here and there. It was a chilly overcast day, typical Normandy weather.

As they marched down the gangway, Trevor tried to picture a hail of bullets all around them. He could almost feel the weight of each GI's equipment, the pack on his back, the grenades at his belt. His hands cradled an imaginary weapon, which he "aimed" at an imaginary enemy way up on the bluff.

He was holding that pose when he noticed her looking at him—a blond girl about his age, maybe a little older. Embarrassed, he lowered the "rifle" and hurried to keep up with G.G. and Dad, his sneakers splashing through about an inch of water before he stepped up onto the very same pebbly beach the old soldier had described.

G.G. strode inland a short ways, stopped, and just stood there, lost in thought.

Trevor's dad approached and put an arm around his grandfather. "You okay, Grandpa?"

The old man was silent for a long time. Finally he said, almost irritably, "They put in a road."

Trevor stepped up on his other side. "I guess that's so they can get the tourist buses in." He indicated two jitney vans that were loading up passengers.

"Come on, Trev," Dad prompted. "Let's give Grandpa a moment with his thoughts."

They started away when G.G. suddenly said, "It was right there."

Trevor stopped. "What was, G.G.?"

The old soldier pointed. "That was where Freddie bought it. Right by that crosswalk."

Trevor was trying to decide if that was a tear in G.G.'s eye or just a trick of the light when he spotted the same blond girl by the breakwater, still watching him.

I must have made a real idiot out of myself, he reflected ruefully, *charging down that ramp playing pretend soldier.*

The Firestones ended up using that road about an hour later, when they took a short taxi ride back to their rental car. G.G. had the cabbie pull up on the curb in order to avoid driving over the crosswalk. Dad was pleading with his grandfather to "let the poor man do his job." But Trevor understood perfectly.

The crosswalk was where Freddie Altman had stepped on that mine. To G.G., it was hallowed ground.

The day was a blur of museums, historical sites, and monuments dedicated to the invasion of Normandy, Operation Overlord. "Although our part," G.G. pointed out, "hitting the beaches, was actually called Neptune." He shrugged. "The brass hats loved their code names. In my unit, we said every time you went to the latrine it was Operation Look Out Below. And that was the polite version."

G.G. knew everything there was to know about D-Day, even the parts that his unit hadn't been involved in. He explained that while his beach, Omaha, was the site of the fiercest fighting, all the armies met enormous resistance as they continued inland. He showed them Pointe du Hoc, a hundred-foot promontory between Omaha and Utah, where army rangers suffered heavy losses pushing to the top to destroy coastal guns that turned out not to be there. He even had praise for his old enemies the paratroopers when he talked about the village of Sainte-Mère-Église, where an unlucky series of fires in the village lit up thousands of parachutes coming down, and countless lives were lost to snipers.

Late afternoon found the Firestones at the Normandy American Cemetery and Memorial. Dad seemed especially solemn as they walked among the endless rows of immaculate white crosses and the occasional Star of David.

"Makes you think, huh?" Daniel Firestone said to his son. "Battles may look glamorous in movies and on posters, but this is what's left over once the smoke clears away."

"They were all heroes," Trevor said reverently.

"They were kids," Dad amended. "Not much older than you, when you think about it. Every single one of these graves is more than a life lost. It's a family torn apart and generations that will never be born. Look at your great-grandfather. If he'd been killed in the war, neither of us would be standing here right now. Not to mention your kids, and *their* kids, and so on. That's what war's *really* about—pointless destruction."

"It wasn't pointless to save the world from Hitler," Trevor argued.

Dad sighed. "That's just it. We just go from war to war to war. We never seem to learn. Hitler was one of the worst, but there's always someone who wants to take over. Why is it so hard to understand that we have to find a way to live together?"

Trevor turned his attention to his great-grandfather, who was wandering among the markers, reading names as if searching for anyone he might have known.

"You think he's looking for Freddie?" Trevor mused. "Maybe I should show him how to use the computer to find someone. You know how he feels about 'newfangled gadgets.'"

"Maybe we should just let him wander," Dad replied thoughtfully. "This whole Normandy visit has been hard on him emotionally."

Trevor didn't reply, but he couldn't have disagreed more. Dad just didn't get it. Sure, G.G. lost friends on D-Day—especially Freddie—and he was sad about that. But being a part of Operation Overlord was the greatest accomplishment in the old man's life. The way G.G. had taken out that machine-gun nest on Omaha Beach was the coolest thing Trevor had ever heard of outside of a video game. And that wasn't even what he was in France to be honored for. Trevor couldn't wait to hear the full story of how Bravo Company had liberated Sainte-Régine. It was going to be epic!

G.G. bent close to a marker to read the inscription. Trevor blinked. As the old man ducked down, he revealed a slight figure a few rows past him. It was the blond girl! She must have been here with her family, visiting the same handful of Normandy attractions. Only—considering their paths had been crisscrossing all day, he couldn't remember seeing any parents with her.

Eventually, G.G. rejoined them. "I found Freddie," he reported matter-of-factly. "I suppose this is as good a place for him as any."

They returned to the rental car, anxious to get back to their hotel in Cherbourg before dark.

"Hey—" Trevor nodded in the direction of the Citroën. "What's that?"

There on the windshield lay a bundle of gray feathers. Dad picked it up. It was a dead bird, its eyes glassy, its tiny feet hanging limp.

"Our luck," G.G. put in. "It had to land on our car."

"Poor little guy." Dad walked over to the side of the road and placed the bird on some soft grass.

Trevor said nothing. But if the bird had simply died and fallen on the car by sheer random chance, why had it been held in place by one of the Citroën's windshield wipers?

CHAPTER FIFTEEN

OUTSIDE COLOMBIÈRES, FRANCE— APRIL 30

It was like driving through a tunnel, dark and dingy, even on a bright, sunny day. The fields of Normandy were all bordered by hedgerows instead of fences. The hedges—planted on raised berms to begin with—were so dense and so high that the tops of the trees met in a canopy over the narrow two-lane road that had once been paved . . . maybe.

Clutching the wheel with white knuckles, Dad struggled to navigate via a phone that kept losing touch with the GPS. When they met another car coming in the opposite direction, it was a nerve-racking squeeze.

"Tell me again why we came this way," he said through clenched teeth. "There are perfectly good roads all over France. Why are we on this one?"

"Trevor wanted to see where I was during the war," G.G. replied. "This is it."

"On this road?" Trevor asked.

"Hedgerow country," the old soldier explained. "There's nothing quite like it anywhere else in the world."

Trevor looked around. "What's so special about the woods?"

"Pull over," G.G. ordered his grandson.

"What—here?"

Impatiently, the old man reached down and yanked up the Citroën's parking brake. With a screech, the car fishtailed to a halt.

"Grandpa!" Dad exclaimed. "You can't just—"

G.G. swung his long legs out the door, climbed up the berm, and, before their horrified eyes, began ramming himself through the dense foliage. In a few gargantuan efforts, he had vanished.

"Awesome!" Trevor ran up the earthen boundary and tried to bull his way through the vegetation where he'd seen his great-grandfather disappear. It wasn't like any bush he'd ever encountered. The hedgerow consisted of shrubs and trees that had been growing there for centuries. Some of the trunks were the thickness of a person's waist or even larger.

"Trevor! Grandpa!" Dad's agitated voice rang out.

A hand reached back through the greenery, grasped Trevor by the arm, and hauled him through. A branch scraped painfully across his face as he joined G.G. on the other side. He was in a field about the size of a football gridiron, but oddly shaped, with angles nowhere near ninety degrees. It was freshly plowed and ready for planting, bound on all sides by the towering, overgrown hedgerows.

"You guys, where are you?" came a plaintive voice through the shrubbery. A moment later, the leaves parted and Dad burst through. He rolled down the berm and landed at their feet.

Trevor helped his father back up. "How'd you know about this place, G.G.?"

"Know it? I crawled through most of it. This part of the world is so old that they've been growing their own fences since time began. Fighting in this stuff was one of the biggest miscalculations of the whole war. We were supposed to be out of hedgerow country in a day. You know how long it took? More than two weeks."

Trevor was mystified. "Why?"

G.G. indicated the dense growth all around them. "These hedgerows—they may look pretty in the aerial photographs, but they're murder for fighting. You can't drive a tank through them!"

"I thought you can drive a tank through anything," Trevor protested. "In video games, you can drive a tank through a brick wall."

"This stuff is stronger than a brick wall. Not to mention that the place is paradise for a defending army to dig in. A single gun emplacement on one of these berms could hold off a division. And if by some miracle you get through that, there's another hedgerow across the next field. According to the army, this place averages fourteen hedgerows per kilometer. And the generals couldn't understand why we were making such slow progress."

"Messieurs, messieurs!" A middle-aged man slipped through the hedge with ease and skill, like an old pro. Over one arm he carried a wicker basket.

He approached G.G. *"Américain?"* he asked, then translated himself. "You are American?"

G.G. nodded. "How'd you know?"

"Ah." The Frenchman nodded back. "A man your age,

visiting these fields. You were once a soldier here, *n'est-ce pas?*"

The old man stuck out his hand. "Jacob Firestone."

The farmer clutched it in both fists and shook it emotionally. "It is my honor to have you on my farm, monsieur. My *grand-père* often spoke of the American heroes who came to free our land." He pulled the basket from his shoulder. "A gift for you—*un cadeau*. You must be hungry. Please enjoy. And thank you one time more."

"Wow, G.G.," Trevor whispered as the farmer magically disappeared into his hedge. "Were all the French this grateful?"

"Not always," the old soldier admitted. "Like when we had to shell the Germans out of their towns. Sometimes there wasn't much town left to liberate."

Dad was the practical one. "Let's see what's in the basket. I'm starving!"

The farmer's gift turned out to be a picnic lunch of crusty French bread, a slab of fresh cheese, and bottles of cool spring water. In no time at all, they were perched atop the berm, chowing down and loving it.

Munching contentedly, Trevor peered over his shoulder through the foliage of the hedge into the next field. He closed his eyes and tried to picture Bravo Company in 1944 slogging through these endless hedgerows, never knowing when their deadly enemy might be waiting on the other side.

CHAPTER SIXTEEN

OUTSIDE COLOMBIÈRES, FRANCE— JUNE 14, 1944

"The tank's stuck."

"Don't be an idiot," Jacob mumbled around a piece of chocolate from his field rations. "Tanks don't get stuck."

Beau grabbed him by the collar and hauled him upright. "Look!"

A Sherman tank was halfway up the berm, grinding and groaning, making no progress against the thick trunks of the hedge at the top. Soldiers ran for cover as the spinning treads kicked up a blizzard of mud, dirt, and torn roots. Several cows looked on, unimpressed by the presence of soldiers, heavy weapons, and even tanks in their pasture. Normandy must be dairy country, because there seemed to be cows everywhere. How the farmers managed to get their cattle through the hedges to be milked was something the US Army never quite figured out. Where could a cow go that a tank couldn't? It was just another baffling aspect of a very baffling war.

"Back it down!" bellowed Sergeant Rajinsky, who had taken over the platoon until the wounded Lieutenant McCoy was able to return to duty.

The Sherman retreated down the berm, veered about ten

meters to the left, and tried to break through at a different spot. It was another no-go.

"They say First Infantry has spear-shaped plow attachments for their Shermans that cut right through the hedgerows," Leland put in. "Why can't we get that?"

"Why?" Jacob said disgustedly. "It's the army. When's the last time they did something that made sense? A whole continent to invade, and they picked here."

It was the kind of complaining that had characterized their training since Fort Benning. But now, at D-Day plus eight, it had taken on a bitter undertone. Bravo Company was down to barely 120 men. Of the casualties, 28 had been killed. It was not lost on Jacob, Beau, and Leland that a few days ago, their friend Freddie would have been a part of this conversation, bellyaching as loud as any of them.

Eventually, half the platoon was involved in a spirited debate on how to get through the hedge. Rajinsky decided to use the tank to blow an opening for itself into the next field.

"Won't that tell the Germans we're coming?" Leland queried.

"I think they figured that out," Jacob put in. "On D-Day."

"If there are Germans around here," Rajinsky concluded, "they've already heard us. Shermans don't have mufflers, you know."

So the tank fired two rounds directly into the top of the berm, opening up a gap about twelve feet wide. Instantly, a hail of machine-gun fire came sizzling through the breach, beating a drum solo on the tank's armor, sending bullets ricocheting in all directions. A fragment struck a glancing blow on Jacob's helmet, and he dropped to the grass, dazed.

"High School!" Beau raced to his side. "You hit?"

"Just got my bell rung," Jacob managed. He glanced up into the black-and-white face of a mildly interested cow. "What are you looking at, Elsie?"

Beau heaved a sigh of relief. "I'm definitely sticking with you. You've got nine lives!"

The Sherman rolled over what was left of the berm and through the gap, the platoon advancing cautiously behind it. They could see no Germans firing at them, but they fired back anyway, peppering the far hedge with a deadly barrage. The tank blasted away, toppling tree trunks and pulverizing the next berm. More explosions came from a mortar emplacement two fields back, raining shells down onto the enemy positions. The sound was a never-ending roar of *ratatat* punctuated by *boom*.

The troops fanned out to the edges of the field, squatting as deep into the hedges as they could insert themselves. They'd gotten good at this kind of fighting, but Jacob never got used to it. Every now and then a handful of men would duck out of their hiding places, advance a few feet, and duck back in again. They dared go no farther at any one time. Their priority was to keep the Germans pinned down so they couldn't take aim. But one look at the bullet holes perforating the surrounding trees was enough to convince Jacob that the reason he was still alive was sheer random chance. Or perhaps fate. Maybe today just wasn't his day to die.

Jacob blinked. The sun peeked out from behind a cloud,

glinting off something smooth and black at the base of the berm. The enemy sometimes tunneled into the mounds from behind, exposing only the muzzles of their machine guns.

"MG!" he bellowed at the top of his lungs, shooting at the spot with his rifle. Bullets ripped into the earth and roots of the berm, but the muzzle continued to spit flame. How could he reach an enemy who was protected by inches of ancient dirt and woody roots?

The tank supplied the answer. It slammed a shell into the gun dead-on. The muzzle vanished, along with most of the berm, and the shrubs and trees growing out of it.

The combat raged on. Bravo Company had the advantage, but the enemy made them bleed for every inch they took. The Germans had been in Normandy for years, and knew exactly how to defend hedgerow country. Men fell, picked off by sniper and machine-gun fire.

Everyone was bathed in sweat and covered in mud, foliage, and wood chips when Rajinsky radioed to end the mortar barrage and signaled his men to cease firing. The battle was over—at least for this field. There was a virtually identical field just beyond what was left of the hedge, and another one beyond that. And so on, and so on.

Bravo had lost two men. Seven others were wounded.

This time, the Sherman had no trouble finding a place to drive over the hedgerow. It had opened several suitable spots during the course of the fighting.

It was only after crossing to the next field that the platoon met their enemies—in a manner of speaking. Their lifeless bodies were strewn across the trenches they had dug on the opposite side of the berm. A few slumped in foxholes.

Rajinsky did a quick head count and came up short. "Not enough," he reported. "You know what that means."

Jacob nodded. "They'll be waiting for us in the next field."

"Or the one after that," Beau added grimly.

That was the thing about the hedgerows, Jacob reflected. You felt like you were wandering through an endless labyrinth, and every time you fought through a new opening, a new wall blocked your way.

But it was worse than that. At least in a labyrinth, nobody was shooting at you.

CHAPTER SEVENTEEN

SAINT-LÔ, FRANCE—APRIL 30

"You've been quiet, Trev," Daniel Firestone tossed over his shoulder as he drove the rental car south through the Normandy countryside toward the town of Saint-Lô.

Trevor couldn't quite put his finger on it, but something had been bugging him ever since their picnic lunch. "I'm okay," he said vaguely, sounding not okay at all.

G.G. was not fooled. "Out with it, kid. What's on your mind?"

"It's that battle of the hedgerows you talked about." Trevor struggled to put his feelings into words. "I get that it happened and all that. But it just doesn't sound, you know, *war* enough."

The old soldier laughed mirthlessly. "Let me assure you it was war enough. For a lot of good men, it was too much war. They never came home from *bocage* country."

"Yeah, I understand that," Trevor conceded. "But shooting at an enemy you can't see. Using a tank to blow up bushes. Fighting one field at a time with a few dozen guys. I mean, a hundred and fifty thousand soldiers landed on D-Day and more were coming every minute. Where were they all?"

"They were in their own fields, trying to get their own tanks unstuck," G.G. replied reasonably. He motioned out the window at the passing scenery. "I'm sure you noticed that they never run out of fields around here."

"I guess," Trevor admitted. "But it just seems wrong. In video games, war is huge crazy battles, with ginormous explosions and everybody fighting full-on."

"Maybe somebody should have pointed out to you," Dad put in sarcastically, "that video games aren't the same as real life. Oh, wait. Somebody tried to. But you wouldn't listen to me."

"The battles were every bit as big as your video games," G.G. assured his great-grandson. "But when you're in the middle of it, it's personal and small. Your job is all that matters. The covering fire you have to lay down. The foxhole you have to dig. The fifty meters you have to run to make it to where you're supposed to be. You're one tiny pawn in a giant chess game, but you're important too. If you don't achieve your little objective, the whole plan could fall apart."

"Even when your job is a field of cows?" Trevor asked dubiously.

"Forget the cows. They were just civilians. Look, we're coming up on Saint-Lô. That was the center of Operation Cobra, which was the turning point of the whole invasion."

"Now, that's more like it," Trevor said approvingly.

"It was a huge operation," the old man went on, "but every soldier still fought his own war. We did our job so General Patton's Third Army could break out of Normandy and roll across France. And we couldn't have managed that if the Canadians and the Brits hadn't been keeping half the German units pinned down to the north in Caen. And remember, all those armies were just hundreds of thousands of regular fellows like me, each with his own little assignment."

"And what was your assignment, G.G.?" Trevor probed.

"Mostly trying not to get blown up. The air corps bombed us by mistake. Or maybe we were in the wrong place. Who knows? But let me tell you, it doesn't feel like friendly fire when it's coming down on your head. And those flyboys—they can't hear what you're yelling up at them. Good thing too, or they would have bombed us twice as hard."

"Here's Saint-Lô now." Dad pointed to a sign as the Citroën drove by.

"Wait—" Trevor was astonished. "We're here *already*? This is the place it took you two months of fighting to get to?"

G.G. shrugged. "We weren't dawdling. The Germans were real stingy about what they'd let us have. That's why they call it a war. There are two sides. We found out later that the order came from Hitler himself to defend Normandy to the last man. I give them credit. They pretty much did that—until Saint-Lô."

Trevor wasn't sure what he'd been expecting, but Saint-Lô looked more like a small bustling city than the village among the hedgerows his great-grandfather had described. The downtown was dominated by a cathedral called Notre-Dame de Saint-Lô, surrounded by neighborhoods of modern buildings and streets of shops.

That was the thing—it all seemed new, or at least newish. "G.G., I thought you said the towns in Normandy were really old."

"They must have done a lot of rebuilding," his great-grandfather concluded. "Because when we left it, it was flat as a pancake."

"This is a perfect example of the destructive power of war," Dad added from the driver's seat. "I'll bet the people of Saint-Lô didn't ask to have their town at the flashpoint of a giant war."

"They should have been *happy*," Trevor argued. "They were liberated from the Nazis! Right, G.G.?"

The old man's gaze turned far away as he remembered. "They were—sort of. We freed the place—what was left of it. But they were the ones who had to rebuild pretty much from the Stone Age."

"Can you imagine that happening to Marlborough?" Dad put in.

Trevor tried to picture his own hometown bombed to rubble, but the image just wouldn't come. Marlborough had always been there. And in his mind, it always would be. Then again, the kids in Saint-Lô had probably thought the same thing.

"Yeah, but think how much time we'd get off school," he shot back. "They close every time it snows."

That drew an appreciative laugh from his great-grandfather. "Good one, kid! Always look on the bright side!"

The Hôtel de Petites Fleurs was located just a couple of blocks from the cathedral on a broad avenue of shops, restaurants, and cafés. The hotel was smaller than where they'd stayed in Cherbourg, but the clientele was similar. A lot of the guests sitting around the lobby were men about G.G.'s age. It had been three-quarters of a century, yet the war still cast its shadow over France. These people were probably on the same pilgrimage as the Firestones. They and their families were retracing their steps from the D-Day beaches across Europe. Some of them wore hats bearing the insignia of legendary fighting units like the American Big Red One or the British Twenty-First Army Group. Eventually, they would disperse as they followed their various units into the heart of Europe. But here in Normandy, they were close together. For Trevor it was an eye-opener. The scope of the fighting force that had landed in France in 1944 was practically too vast to contemplate. How General Eisenhower, the supreme Allied commander, had managed to keep track of it all was a miracle.

Up in their suite, while the old soldier settled himself down for a nap, Trevor used his phone to call up pictures of Saint-Lô from before the war. He stalked from window to window, trying to match the view to the old photographs. Except for the cathedral, there was nothing recognizable. How had G.G. described it? *Flat as a pancake.* It really must have been. In video games, your own air raids and artillery barrages always seemed okay. But they knocked down buildings and ruined cities every bit as mercilessly as the enemy's firepower.

Dad reclined in an armchair, scrolling through Facebook. For a guy who always complained that Trevor spent too much time online, he'd certainly become obsessed with social media ever since this trip had started. Maybe he was searching for a good restaurant for tonight's dinner. There were probably a lot of options now that Saint-Lô had turned into such a tourist town.

Trevor was at the glass again, trying to line up rue du Belle with the image on his phone, when he spied her. She was looking up at the hotel from window to window when her eyes met his.

It was the blond girl from Omaha Beach. Trevor bristled. This was more than a coincidence. Why was she turning up everywhere the Firestones went?

She stared at him for a long second, then broke away to hurry off down the street.

Trevor ran for the door. "Be right back," he tossed over his shoulder.

Dad was mystified. "Where are you going?"

But Trevor was already pounding down the hall. Not willing to wait for the elevator, he took the stairs three at a time and burst out the front door onto the street. At first, he couldn't spot her in the crowded square. Then he caught a glimpse of her green hoodie, hurrying around a corner. Turning on the afterburners, he sprinted up behind her and touched her shoulder. "Hey—"

With a gasp, she wheeled around. It wasn't her. It wasn't even a kid. It was a woman in her twenties with a nose ring and a face tattoo.

"Sorry!" he stammered. "I thought you were some-body else."

She mumbled something in French and marched off.

Trevor pivoted away, desperately scanning faces. How could she have disappeared so fast? He had to find her. It was the only way to get to the bottom of this.

The sound of a car horn attracted his attention to the far end of the block. There she was, on the opposite side of the square, hurrying away.

Trevor began to push his way in her direction, calling, "Come back!"

There were complaints from the people in his way. A few muttered, *"Américains!"*

The blond girl never turned around, not even when he broke through the throng and shouted, "I just want to talk!"

She definitely heard him. He could see her shoulders stiffen. But she increased her pace.

At the next intersection, a motorcycle pulled up in front of her and stopped. She climbed aboard behind the driver, a slim male figure. She pulled on a helmet and they drove off. A few seconds later, they were out of sight.

An older lady told him, in English, "Do not worry, young man. There will be other girls for you."

"No, it's not that. It's—" How could he ever explain it? "Thanks," he mumbled, starting back across the square.

By the time he got to the hotel, both Dad and G.G. were waiting for him in the lobby.

Dad looked like he was about to organize a search party. "What was that all about, Trev? Where did you go?"

Even his normally unflappable great-grandfather was concerned. "You're halfway around the world, mister. You can't just go skylarking around town whenever it suits you."

"But this is serious!" Breathlessly, he told them about the girl, and how she'd been reappearing ever since Omaha Beach.

"How is it that she turns up wherever we happen to be? It's like she's following us!"

G.G. made a face. "Last time I was in France, there were a lot of blonds following me. They were called Germans and every single one of them was trying to kill me."

"I know it looks that way, but she's *not* following you," Dad explained patiently. "We're just over a week away from the seventy-fifth anniversary of V-E Day. France is full of old soldiers and their families, all doing exactly what we're doing."

"So don't yell *bingo* in a crowded room," G.G. chortled. "Not unless you want to start a riot."

"It can't be a coincidence," Trevor argued. "It's not just that she's everywhere. She's looking at me. Just now she was staring directly into our room."

"Did it ever occur to you that she thinks *you're* following *her*?" G.G. suggested. "You're not the only one who can recognize a familiar face."

"I don't mean to shoot down everything you say," Dad told Trevor. "But it just doesn't make sense. Why would this girl give two hoots about us? We're tourists like everybody else—probably including her."

"What about that dead bird on our car?" Trevor challenged. "If that was a message, it wasn't a very friendly one."

"Enough of this," G.G. interrupted. "I've been to Saint-Lô twice, and it's hard to say which visit had more fighting in it. Let's go out and see this town. We leave for Paris in the morning."

They walked all around Saint-Lô and then toured the

cathedral and its museum. Trevor was amazed by the before-and-after photographs showing the devastation of the Gothic cathedral. An entire stone tower had been knocked down by Allied bombs.

"Don't blame me," G.G. whispered. "I wasn't in the air corps. It's a miracle they didn't blow me up along with the church."

Dad was most interested in the architecture, art, and stained glass windows. He was determined to make this trip educational or die trying, but Trevor didn't care about naves, apses, and vaulted ceilings. He had to admit, though, that the people of Saint-Lô had done a great job restoring a building that had been virtually reduced to rubble.

Dad must have thought that was enough education for one day, because he let G.G. and Trevor outvote him on the traditional French restaurant and have pizza for dinner. But he insisted on ending the evening at an outdoor café, despite the old soldier's opinion that "the coldest winter I ever spent in my life was the summer I spent in Normandy." It was exactly that kind of night—chilly and damp, with a biting wind. They sat shivering in their jackets, trying to enjoy ice cream that was only slightly colder than the air.

The next morning, the Firestones were up with the sunrise. Paris was almost three hundred kilometers away, and they were anxious to get an early start.

They gathered up their luggage and headed for the parking lot.

Somehow, their car looked different. Wrong. Out of balance.

"The front's too low," Trevor observed.

"Or the back's too high," G.G. added.

When they reached the Citroën, the problem was obvious. Both front tires had been slashed. The vehicle leaned forward, resting on the rims.

The three glanced around at the other vehicles in the lot. Theirs was the only one damaged.

"Who would do such a thing?" Dad demanded.

Trevor thought of the mysterious blond girl and her accomplice on the motorcycle.

CHAPTER EIGHTEEN

OUTSIDE SAINT–JEAN–DE–DAYE, FRANCE—JULY 25, 1944

Dear Ma and Pa,

How are you? I am writing to you from a foxhole in . . .

"Hey, Beau," Jacob called over to his friend in the foxhole a few meters away. "Where in France are we?"

"Doesn't matter, High School," came Beau's reply. "You can't give away anything about where you are. The censors will just black it out."

"Fine," Jacob grumbled. "I'll just tell them I'm working hard not to get run over by our own tanks."

"Uh-uh. Can't say that either. Hitler might want to know what equipment we've got."

Jacob was disgusted. "Well, what *can* I say? *Having a nice war; wish you were here?*"

Beau stuck his head out of his foxhole. "Will you shut up? I'm writing my own letter to Kitty. You think it's easy to be romantic knowing that some officer with a leg full of shrapnel and a blank inkpad is going to be drooling over it?"

"Ask your mom to send cookies," Leland piped up from another hole.

"And send them where?" Jacob demanded. "General Delivery—Europe?"

"There is no General Delivery," Beau rumbled. "We've got an Eisenhower, a Bradley, a Patton—"

"Ben Schwartz's mother sent a salami from Brooklyn and it found him just fine," Leland argued. "First Platoon had heartburn for a week."

"Maybe it came with the ammo," Jacob mused. "They probably thought it was a torpedo."

Lieutenant McCoy, newly recovered from his D-Day injuries, strode among the foxholes. "Pack up, men. We're moving out."

Cries of protest rose from the ground all around him.

"Moving out?" Leland echoed. "Battalion said to dig in and get a few hours' sleep."

"I know," the officer shot back. "I'm the one they told it to. Now they want us on the move again."

There was no shortage of grumbling, but the men of Bravo Company were out of their foxholes and ready to go in a matter of minutes. The past seven weeks had been a whirlwind of firefights, troop movements, and, occasionally, a rare chance to drop back for a meal and a rest. Sometimes they would be on the go for as long as three days and nights. The exhaustion was so constant that it had become their normal state. Jacob had learned to sleep in a foxhole, or even standing up during a break on a long march. He could take apart his rifle, clean it, and put it back together again while not completely awake.

Without regular sleep, the days and nights blurred together. In some ways, the seven weeks of near-constant fighting felt like much less. Yet basic training at Fort Benning might as well have been in another life. Jacob could get used to all of it—except the combat. When bullets were flying and shells bursting, his heart would beat so hard and so fast that he feared it might explode out of his chest. Those moments—sometimes hours; sometimes whole days—were so loud, so chaotic, so violent that they almost belonged to another universe. Then someone close by would be hit—wounded or killed—and reality would intrude once more.

When Jacob closed his eyes, the picture of what bullets or shrapnel could do to a human being was never far away. He had already seen more death than he'd ever imagined possible. And more blood—it was hard to believe there could be so much of it. At times, he had found himself surrounded by so many bodies—from both sides in this war—that it became difficult to remember that these had once been *people*. Brothers and sons. Husbands and fathers and friends . . .

Friends. The word was a sucker punch to Jacob's gut.

Freddie.

Like a scratched record jumping back to the same discordant note, that horrible moment on Omaha Beach played over and over in Jacob's brain. The crack of the detonating mine. The unbelieving look on Freddie's face just before he was launched skyward.

And then . . .

Don't think about it! Jacob commanded himself. That shattered body was *not* his buddy. Not Freddie, with his open, comfortable face and warm, easy laugh.

But every time Jacob let himself remember the Freddie from Fort Benning or Petersfield, the image soon shifted. Freddie, lifeless on Omaha Beach.

Freddie who would never be Freddie again.

Despite his exhaustion, Jacob was almost grateful for the order to move out.

Some memories were too awful to dwell upon.

Bravo Company was on the go again, trying to stay alert, watchful.

"I miss the tanks," Leland said wanly. "That's the best place to be when the shooting starts—right behind something big and armored."

"Are you crazy?" Beau countered. "A Sherman is like a gigantic green target. Give me a good hiding place every time."

The conversation went back and forth about the pros and cons of tanks as they marched along a country lane. It wasn't long before Jacob had the sense that some kind of battle had taken place not far from there—fallen leaves and branches, singed grasses, broken wires hanging from poles.

Eventually, they reached the site of the fighting—a tiny village, perhaps six or seven buildings in all. It was empty of inhabitants. The people of Normandy had gotten good at leaving town before the war reached them. There wasn't a single window that hadn't been shattered by gunfire, and a couple of walls had collapsed due to mortar shells or grenades. The locals had made the right decision to desert their homes.

Jacob reached down and picked up a German helmet. There was a bullet hole through the side, but otherwise the metal was shiny and perfect, as if it had just come from the factory. The inside was caked with dried blood. He dropped it quickly and moved on.

In a field beyond the town, a crashed plane lay with its nose half buried in the tilled earth. As the company continued along the lane, Jacob scrambled to a gap in the hedge for a better look. It was a fighter, a British Mustang.

"Hurry up, High School," Beau called.

Jacob was about to jump back down the berm when something inside the cockpit moved. "Lieutenant!" he shouted. "There's somebody in that plane! Somebody alive!"

He jumped down to the field and ran toward the plane. When he reached the cockpit, he found a pair of eyes peering out at him, and even a smiling face. He was greeted by a very British "Hello."

Because of the impact of the crash, the pilot was trapped in his seat, his legs pressed forward under the smashed instrument panel. The smell of leaking fuel was almost overpowering.

"Are you all right?" Jacob asked.

"Just a little spot of bother," the Englishman acknowledged.

By this time, Beau, Leland, and several others were hightailing it across the field to offer their help.

The cockpit door had jammed, so they had to pry it open with their shovels. Jacob and Beau took hold of the Englishman from under his arms and pulled him free of the wreckage. When they set him down, he took one wobbly step and collapsed.

"Blimey," he observed. "My leg's been shot through with anti-aircraft fire."

Beau was amazed. "And you're just noticing that now?"

"My foot was asleep," he explained. "It was trapped under the rudder bar when I crashed." He looked back at his plane. "Well, that's seen better days."

"How long have you been here?" Jacob asked.

"That would depend. What's the date today?"

"July twenty-fifth," Leland supplied.

The pilot frowned. "I say! That would be three days without food or water. Plus blood loss from the leg—" He keeled over, unconscious.

🚶 🚶 🚶 🚶

It took less than an hour for battalion to send an ambulance to pick up the rescued British pilot. By that time, the flight lieutenant had downed three canteens of water and two chocolate bars, and was chatting with Bravo Company like they were old friends. He seemed genuinely dismayed when the medics came to take him away from such a "grand bunch of Yanks."

As the ambulance pulled out, Lieutenant McCoy cast Jacob a swift nod. "Nice catch."

Moments like this made Jacob feel good about his decision to walk into that recruiting center more than a year ago. It was true that in this war, he was nothing more than a tiny cog in a vast machine. But he could still make a difference.

The company resumed its progress south. Several times, they had to leave the road to allow armored and mechanized columns to pass them. At intersections among the hedgerows, other infantry units joined them, until thousands of soldiers were all marching in the same direction.

"Big party," Beau observed.

"My invitation must have gotten lost in the mail," Jacob put in.

"Oh, we're invited, all right," Beau assured him. "The army insists."

As the troops mingled on their movement south, bits of information passed from mouth to mouth. Some of these were obviously rumors, and pretty wild ones at that: the war was almost over; they'd be home in two weeks; Hitler had abandoned Berlin and was holed up in a farmhouse somewhere. But amid the unbelievable stories, one word rose above all others: Cobra.

"I'm afraid of snakes," Leland volunteered. "Ever since I was two and a grass snake bit me."

"This isn't a real snake," Beau said impatiently. "It's one of those code names the brass hats are so crazy about. Operation Cobra."

"Another plot to get us all killed" was Leland's opinion.

"If what everybody's saying is true, we're breaking out of

Normandy," Jacob offered. "Can't be too soon for me. If I never see another hedgerow, that's just fine."

By late afternoon, Bravo Company had left the procession and was draped in various poses around an abandoned farm, consuming field rations. In the distance, they could see the single tower of a ruined cathedral.

"That's Saint-Lô," Sergeant Rajinsky told them. "That church used to have two steeples, but the air corps knocked one of them down on D-Day."

"Now we know what happened to our air support at Omaha," Jacob commented. "They were in the wrong place, bombing churches."

Rajinsky favored him with a crooked grin. "Any time you're feeling sorry for yourself, remember the people of Saint-Lô. They got flattened by us on D-Day. They got bombed by the Germans. And guess where the generals have decided Operation Cobra should be." He checked his wristwatch. "They're going to get it again in about twenty minutes. Poor Frenchies."

It was typical of the military. Bombs meant for the coast might fall on a cathedral fifty kilometers inland, but when an air raid was scheduled for 1742 hours, it would not happen at 1743.

Right on schedule, two spotter planes appeared in the sky above Saint-Lô and fired flares over the town. Almost immediately, a squadron of dive-bombers came streaking overhead. Puffs of anti-aircraft fire bloomed all around them.

"Those flyboys, they're something else," Jacob commented admiringly.

The bombs began to fall, a series of distant rumbles that blended into a general roar.

Pretty soon, Saint-Lô disappeared under a pall of flame-tinged smoke. Only the single church tower was still visible through the billowing clouds, which blew across the fields in their direction.

"Oh, great," Beau complained. "Now we have to breathe it."

But the onslaught wasn't over yet. The earth began to vibrate and an approaching hum grew into a painful buzzing in their ears.

Leland pointed. "Look!"

A squadron of heavy bombers filled the air, moving in such tight formation that they looked like a pattern on wallpaper. Bravo Company watched their approach until the windborne smoke from Saint-Lô obscured the spectacle in the sky.

And then the first explosion came from the second wave—far too close. The bomb hit just a few hundred meters to the south of them, sending a huge geyser of earth and brush straight up.

"Incoming!" bellowed Rajinsky.

The company scattered, scrambling for any kind of cover on the abandoned farm. Jacob pulled on his helmet and sprinted for the farmhouse. At that moment, a second bomb hit, blowing the stone structure to tiny pieces. A rock the size of a cantaloupe sailed past his left ear, and he was battered with dust and mortar debris. The blast knocked him flat on his back, and for a moment, he lay there, stunned. Then he was being dragged by the arms through the open door of the barn. Beau and Leland. They were shouting at him urgently, but now the bombs were falling in a nonstop barrage, and he couldn't hear what they were saying.

The three of them crawled under a buckboard and huddled there, praying that the heavy wooden cart would be strong enough to protect them. A moment later, another body squirmed in beside them. Rajinsky.

"Why are they bombing their own guys?" Leland howled in terror.

"They don't know it's us!" the sergeant bellowed back. "All they can see is the smoke from the first wave."

For more than an hour, American and British bombers pounded Saint-Lô. And for more than an hour, far too many of those bombs fell on the little farm where Bravo Company had stopped for a meal break. The noise was unlike anything Jacob had ever experienced before, even on D-Day. It went beyond hearing—it was a physical presence. He felt each explosion in his vital organs and in the gums beneath his teeth. The earth shook with each blast, rattling his brain inside his skull. It was impossible to think, even to be afraid—although on some level he understood that if one of those bombs scored a direct hit on the barn, he and his companions would be blown to bits. There was a time during the barrage that he even toyed with the possibility that he might be better off that way. At least then the torture would be over.

It was impossible to tell when the bombing stopped. The entire company had gone temporarily deaf, and the reverberations continued in their minds long after the air raid had ended.

When the four of them climbed out from under the

buckboard, they found themselves buried in shattered pieces of lumber. The whole ghastly experience had been so loud that none of them had noticed the barn collapsing around them. If it hadn't been for the shelter of the buckboard, they would surely have been crushed.

It took some doing for the four soldiers to dig their way out of the wreckage of the barn. At that, they needed several platoon-mates heaving splintered boards off of them. Jacob emerged to find a world he barely recognized as the place he'd had his field rations an hour earlier.

The farm was gone. Not a single structure remained. Not a field was left undamaged. Craters twelve feet in diameter and four feet deep dotted the landscape like chicken pox. One bomb had blasted a twenty-foot gap in a hedgerow, scattering trees, bushes, and heavy tangles of roots. Smoke hung in the air, along with the acrid smell of gunpowder, burnt earth, and concrete dust.

Medics scrambled everywhere, tending to the wounded. Two bodies were covered by crimson-stained blankets. Close to the rubble of the house, a jeep was flipped over and burning.

"Our own air corps," Jacob said aloud.

Beau and Leland regarded him questioningly and he realized they were deafened and couldn't hear him. He could barely hear himself.

"Our own air corps did this," Jacob repeated, practically shouting just to register his own voice. "With friends like them, who needs the Germans?"

Leland nodded his bitter agreement. "We're suffering when the enemy is getting off scot-free!"

"I don't think so." Beau pointed through the dispersing smoke in the direction of Saint-Lô.

The smoke over the town glowed bright orange. Leaping tongues of flame showed over the horizon. The entire place was ablaze.

"Looks like they saved some bombs for the bad guys after all," Leland commented, patting at his right ear.

Jacob stared at the burning city. Perhaps a couple dozen bombs had accidentally fallen at the farm, and it had been, by far, the most traumatic experience of his young life. But what must it have been like to be the actual target of all that weaponry?

What was it like for the people of Saint-Lô as wave after wave of death and destruction rained down on them?

CHAPTER NINETEEN

ON THE ROAD TO PARIS, FRANCE—MAY 1

"That can't be true!" Trevor protested. "Why would the planes bomb their own guys? Are you sure you're remembering it right?"

It was early afternoon, and the Firestones were finally on the road to Paris after the rental company had provided two new tires for the Citroën.

G.G. laughed mirthlessly. "Believe me, you don't forget something like that. We lost two guys in the raid, and our wounded couldn't be evacuated until Cobra was over. First things first, you know."

"But that's no good," Trevor insisted. "I understand that soldiers die in battle, but not sitting around on a snack break. And not because their own pilots don't know who's where."

"It's called friendly fire, Trev," Dad put in from behind the wheel.

"It isn't very friendly, but it happens," the old soldier added. "And when it does, you couldn't care less who's shooting at you—the Germans or FDR himself."

"But it's *wrong*." Trevor struggled to put his emotions into words. "I get that war is risky, but the least we can do is make sure our troops don't get killed by *mistake*."

"You're thinking of today—smart bombs, smart weaponry, smart this, smart that. It sounds more like a convention of egg-heads than any battle. Back in the war, we didn't have that stuff. No matter how much you plan and strategize and calculate all the angles, once the shooting starts, it's basically chaos."

"It may be glamorous to imagine fighting an enemy," Dad added. "But bombs and bullets don't care who they hit, and the real enemy is the fighting itself."

"Are you saying war is so bad that we should have just let Hitler take over the world?" Trevor challenged.

Dad paused for a long moment before replying. "Some things are worth fighting for. I'm just saying that it's awful, that's all. Wars may have winning sides, but everybody loses."

Trevor waited for G.G. to break in and tell Dad that he didn't know what he was talking about. But the old man kept his eyes on the passing French countryside and stayed silent.

He perked up later on, when road signs began to mention towns he remembered from the war—Évreux . . . Fauville . . . Miserey.

"I guess you were pretty miserable there, huh?" Trevor wisecracked.

"You said it," G.G. agreed with a grin. "That's where Leland, the dope, got himself bitten by a dog. He thought he had his million-dollar wound—you know, the one that gets you sent home. No such luck. The medics gave him rabies shots all the way to Paris."

Dad was impressed. "I'm surprised the army thought to bring medicine for that."

"Are you kidding? The army thought of everything. They even had ten-gallon barrels of camphorated VapoRub to open up your sinuses after a long day inhaling battlefield stink." He pointed at another sign. "Hey, there's the road to Villegats. We lost Rajinsky there."

Trevor looked solemn. "How did he die?"

"He didn't. He just got lost. We were the first Americans through there, so they threw us a parade, because they thought we were the whole US Army. Rajinsky was looking for a bathroom, but they wouldn't stop kissing him. He had to take a taxi to the next town to catch up with us."

"Kissing him?" That didn't sit well with Trevor's view of the war. "I thought you had to fight your way across France!"

"There was plenty of fighting, believe me," the old soldier assured him. "Back in hedgerow country, you could be dug in for three days just to take one field and six cows. But Cobra was the breakout. We weren't slogging through bushes anymore; we were riding in trucks and jeeps. When there weren't enough spots, we rode on the tanks, eight men to a Sherman, hanging on for dear life. Better than walking, but not much. Because if you fall off the front, the flattest thing in France won't be the crepes."

"But where were the Germans?" Trevor asked.

"They were regrouping—falling farther back into France to solidify their positions. The battles were vicious, but once they were over, we might have fifty klicks of clear sailing ahead. It was whiplash, really—going from slogging over every inch to sailing across the country—*stop the car!*"

Shocked, Dad jammed on the brakes. The Citroën screeched to a halt and almost fishtailed off the road.

"Grandpa! What?"

The old man had raised himself out of his seat, twisting around to peer out the rear window. "Back up! Back up!" he ordered urgently.

"To *where?*"

Trevor was on his knees in the back seat. "Are you talking about that pile of rocks in the ditch?"

G.G. threw open the door, unfolded his long legs out of the Citroën, and began to stride purposefully along the shoulder toward a small structure. Dad and Trevor were hot on his heels.

"Grandpa, where are you going?" Dad called irritably.

When they finally caught up, they found the old man bent over a small stone cistern, drinking water that was bubbling out of an ancient spout.

"Grandpa, that could be poison!" Dad exclaimed.

G.G. looked up, flushed with pleasure. "It wasn't poison seventy-five years ago and it isn't poison now. Help yourself."

Trevor put two and two together. "This has been here— since the war?"

"Probably before that. It was old when we found it. We'd been on the road all day. It was hot, and the captain had us in full gear so we wouldn't lose anything. I've lived ninety-three years and I've never been so uncomfortable. Our canteens were empty. Our field rations were useless. Our mouths were so dry that we couldn't chew anything and swallow it. And then the driver pulled up beside this."

"It must be an underground spring," Dad concluded, "if it's still here after all these years."

"Nothing ever tasted better," the old soldier said with authority. "We drank. We filled our canteens. We ate our rations and we drank some more. From the whole war, my best memory is right here. Try it. You'll go nuts."

Trevor took a sip. It was cold, and tasted very clean and pure. But it was just water. What was the big deal?

So Trevor closed his eyes and pretended he was a battle-weary soldier on a scorching-hot day, exhausted and thirsty. He was bathed in sweat from a firefight that had turned into hand-to-hand combat. His uniform was stained with blood and dirt, his throat baked dry from the heat of the flamethrowers. He took a long drink.

"You're right, G.G. It's the best water I ever tasted."

The old man beamed. "What did I tell you? Can't believe it's still here after seventy-five years. Made my day."

"Seventy-five years isn't very long for a country like this," Dad lectured. "Remember, France dates back to Roman times. This used to be ancient Gaul."

Trevor rolled his eyes at his father. "Another teachable moment, Dad?"

G.G. laughed appreciatively. "You got it, kid. But your old man isn't wrong. In a lot of ways, France isn't that different than it was during the war. Just older—like me. See that grove of trees over there? They were saplings when we stopped here in forty-four. That's where we buried the Iron Cross."

"Iron Cross?" Dad repeated. "The German medal?"

"Hazeltine had one—a machine gunner in our unit. He'd found it on a battlefield a couple of days before. The problem was, he wasn't supposed to keep it. We weren't allowed to collect souvenirs. Battalion had been calling a lot of surprise inspections, and Hazeltine was getting nervous. So while we were stopped here, he took the medal over to those trees and buried it. Third one on the left-hand side."

"And what happened to it?" Trevor asked.

The old soldier shrugged. "How should I know? I haven't been back to check on it."

"I'm going to go see if it's still there!" Trevor was off like a shot, running across the field.

"I hope he doesn't find it," G.G. said quietly. "I don't want to have to explain what Hazeltine did to the German who used to own it."

"Never mind that, Grandpa. I didn't want to talk about it in front of Trevor, but you need to take a look at this Facebook page from Sainte-Régine." Daniel held out his phone.

G.G. made no effort to take it. "I don't hold with all that antisocial media nonsense."

"It's not nonsense, it's this group called La Vérité," Dad insisted. "Someone in that town hates you. I mean *really* hates you."

The old man shrugged. "America doesn't have a monopoly on crackpots, you know. There are bigmouths everywhere, only here they speak French."

His grandson was not convinced. "That was my first thought too—a random complainer, maybe someone who doesn't like Americans. I figured these comments would die out after a while, but they seem to be getting worse as the date approaches. There are at least a dozen new posts every day now. They appear faster than the Sainte-Régine people can delete them. At first, they were all in French, but now they're coming in English too. What do you think that means?"

"I don't care what language they're in—I'm not going to read them" was G.G.'s opinion.

Daniel paused to wave at Trevor, who was on his hands and knees in the grove, scrabbling with his fingers in the earth at the base of the third tree. Absorbed in his digging, Trevor didn't notice him.

"The messages switched to English because *you're* the audience," Trevor's father went on. "And they're getting downright threatening. Listen to this: *'We know the truth about your crimes against Sainte-Régine.' 'If you come here, you'll face vengeance.' 'You will pay for the suffering you caused.'* What do you have to say to that?"

"Sticks and stones," the old man replied. "It's just words."

His grandson was still nervous. "I'm beginning to think it's more than that. Our slashed tires; the dead bird under the windshield wiper. Trev seems to believe that blond girl is stalking us. What if it isn't a figment of his imagination? What if she's mixed up with La Vérité?"

For the first time, his grandfather had no snappy answer. Both men watched as Trevor walked back from the grove of trees, dusting off his hands. G.G. was not intimidated by a few nasty comments on a Facebook page. But the whole thing had to be taken more seriously because Trevor was with them.

"The two of us can protect ourselves, but Trev's twelve," Daniel reasoned. "I don't like the idea of bringing him into the lion's den."

G.G. was adamant. "If you feel like this is too dangerous, then by all means, take the kid and go home. But I'm seeing this through to the end. These threatening messages of yours—they're part of it too. Don't you think I want to find out what it's all about?"

Daniel's eyes narrowed. "Grandpa, do you know something about this that you're not telling me? Something about those messages and who's sending them?"

The old man's eyes flashed. "Do I mind your business?" Then he added, almost to himself, "I didn't think there was anybody left."

"What are you talking about? Who's 'anybody'?"

At that moment, Trevor's voice reached them. "I couldn't find it," he reported briskly. "The ground's too hard to dig with your hands. Maybe we should go to the next town and buy a shovel."

G.G. laughed and shook his head. "No time for that, kiddo. We've got places to go. Next stop: Gay Paree!"

CHAPTER TWENTY

PARIS, FRANCE—MAY 2

Most of the pictures were familiar to the blond girl—Omaha Beach, the historical sites around Normandy, the hedgerows, Saint-Lô. There was one image she couldn't place. It seemed to be an old stone cistern at the side of a road somewhere. Who knew what attracted the attention of these Americans?

Anyway, there was no mistaking the photograph at the top of the Instagram page. Trevor Firestone—who proudly identified himself as the great-grandson of Jacob Firestone, the "hero" of Sainte-Régine. The foolish boy believed that to be related to such a man was something to boast about. For this, Trevor was probably not to be blamed. For sure, his much-adored "G.G." never told him the truth.

Juliette Lafleur scrolled down to the bottom of the Instagram page. It was a picture of the front of the Hôtel Pivoines in Paris. And she knew exactly where it was because she was standing directly across the cobblestoned street from it. Juliette looked up from her phone screen and there it was.

"Here it is," said her tall cousin in French from the seat of his motorcycle.

Philippe was seventeen, four years older than Juliette. This whole thing had been Juliette's idea, but she could not possibly have pulled it off without her cousin. A thirteen-year-old girl never could have traveled all around France on her own. But Philippe had a motorcycle.

"Let's get it done, then," she told him.

Philippe reached into the cargo net under the seat, pulled out a plastic bag, and handed it to Juliette. From it, she removed an exquisitely gift-wrapped box.

"I don't know why we had to make it so pretty," Philippe grumbled, "considering who it's going to."

"It has to look like a present," she explained patiently. "Otherwise, we'll never get it past the front desk."

Juliette tucked the parcel under her arm and headed into the hotel through the automatic doors. Wearing her most innocent expression, she approached the desk and announced in English, "Monsieur Firestone left a key for me."

Juliette knew that none of the three Firestones had done any such thing—not the great-grandfather, the father, nor Trevor. But she kept a sharp eye on the desk clerk as he scanned the wall of pigeonholes behind him. The man reached into the slot for room 407 and came up empty.

"I am sorry, mademoiselle, there is no key for you."

She did her best to look disappointed. "My grand-uncle is no longer a young man. He forgets things. *Merci*." She started for the door. But as soon as the clerk turned his back, she dashed onto the elevator and pressed 4.

On the fourth floor, she marched straight past room 407 to the housekeeping cart, which was parked outside the slightly open door of 419. Inside, she could hear the vacuum cleaner running, which meant she probably had at least a minute or two. She snatched the passkey from the corner of the cart, raced back to 407, let herself into the room, and left the gift package on the carpet just inside the door.

She exited the room to find the maid standing by her cart, gazing around in confusion.

"Is this what you're looking for?" Juliette asked her, handing back the passkey. "I found it on the floor back there."

"Ah, yes. *Merci. Merci.*"

It was only when the elevator door closed behind her that Juliette began to breathe again. How naïve had she and Philippe been to believe that a few Facebook posts would convince Sainte-Régine to cancel their celebration or to scare off this family of Americans?

Perhaps this would be enough to get the job done.

"You know, Trev," Dad said as the weary Firestones returned to their hotel late that afternoon, "Paris has the greatest art museums in the world, including the Louvre. And what are we spending our time looking at? Tanks and guns and pictures of dead and wounded soldiers!"

Trevor was thunderstruck. "Didn't you like the Army Museum? It was *awesome*! Those French Resistance guys had to be the bravest people who ever lived. It's one thing to fight in the army. But with the Resistance, even joining was enough to get you killed!"

As they stepped through the automatic doors, G.G. reached under his shirt collar and pulled out a ring on a thin gold chain. The ring was dull and tarnished compared to the shiny chain. Engraved into the metal was a small cross with two bars.

"That's a Cross of Lorraine!" Trevor exclaimed excitedly. "Symbol of the Resistance!"

Dad spoke up. "Grandpa, you never told me you had anything to do with the Resistance."

"The Resistance was everywhere," G.G. explained. "Especially in Paris. They rose up and started the liberation of the city before we even got here. Toughest fighters I've ever seen. Terrifying if you were a Nazi."

"But who gave you that ring?" Trevor persisted.

"A friend."

"You had a friend in the *Resistance*?" Trevor crowed. "And you didn't tell me?"

"Where is it written that you have to know everything?" his great-grandfather retorted.

Trevor backed up a step. It was the first time he could remember that G.G. had refused to answer one of his questions.

Dad pulled Trevor aside. "Easy, Trev," he said in a low voice. "G.G.'s just tired. There's a lot of walking in these museum visits. It's hard on a man his age."

"I'm not tired and I'm not deaf either," the old soldier tossed over his shoulder as the elevator door opened in front of him.

"I'm going to stay down here and upload the museum pictures to my Instagram," Trevor told him. "There's better Wi-Fi in the lobby. I'll be up in a few minutes."

So Daniel rode to the fourth floor with G.G. They opened the door of room 407 and stared. There on the floor was a festively wrapped package.

The old man was the first to speak. "Well, it's not my birthday . . ."

Daniel bent down and picked it up.

With a bark of anger, G.G. snatched it away from him. "Let me do it! If there's any danger, it's meant for me."

Daniel was nervous again. "If there's any danger, we should be calling the police."

"Well, we won't know that until we open it, will we?" The old soldier ripped away the wrapping paper to reveal a shoebox. Then he tipped up the lid and peered inside.

The first thing he saw was an old-fashioned alarm clock. It was ticking. In a remarkable burst of speed for a man his age, he ran into the bathroom, dumped it in the toilet, and flushed. He held the handle down to keep the water pouring onto the device.

"A bomb?" Dad exclaimed, aghast.

G.G. took a closer look. "Nah. Just a regular alarm clock. Whoever sent it seemed pretty intent on scaring us, though."

"And it worked! I don't mind telling you I'm scared to death!"

The old man examined the empty shoebox and held it up for his grandson to see. Written on the white bottom in Magic Marker were the words:

IT COULD HAVE BEEN REAL

It was signed: *La Vérité.*

In the lobby, Trevor tapped his phone to upload yet another picture. It was of Dad and G.G. posing in front of the desk where the German garrison commander had officially surrendered Paris to Allied forces. G.G. had actually been there on that day in 1944—not in the room with the desk, but outside in the city. That fabulous museum visit had been twice as good thanks to the old man's stories of millions of Parisians celebrating in the streets, heedless of the fact that some renegade Nazi units were still fighting. Nobody cared, because after four years of occupation, Paris had been returned to its people.

Trevor knew he was clogging his Instagram with too many pictures. But how could he leave any of these out? The display cases of guns and weaponry. The Resistance flags—the French tricolor with the Cross of Lorraine in the center. Trevor hoped to add a photograph of the Resistance ring that G.G. was wearing around his neck, but he had a feeling that now was not the time to ask about it. The old soldier was normally cool about everything but for some reason he was sensitive about that ring.

He transferred the last of the pictures—a shot of the outside of the museum in an area called Les Invalides, since it began as a hospital for wounded soldiers. The grounds were swarming with tourists. As the photograph loaded onto Instagram, Trevor's eyes were drawn to the slender figure of a girl. A *blond* girl.

He used his fingers to zoom in, but the image became too blurry.

No way, he told himself. *Now you're seeing things.*

But as he zoomed back out, he noticed that she was walking toward a tall young man on a motorcycle. It was her—*them*. They had been in Saint-Lô. They had been at the beaches of Normandy—or at least *she* had been there. And now they were here in Paris.

Dad had argued that they were just tourists who happened to be on the same World War II route the Firestones were taking. This was different. Paris was a vast city with more attractions for visitors than anyone could count. The presence of this pair at the very same museum on the very same day had to be more than a coincidence.

Who are they and why are they following us? Trevor wondered.

CHAPTER TWENTY-ONE

PARIS, FRANCE—AUGUST 25, 1944

Private Jacob Firestone rolled into Paris on a tank.

There was no other way to get into the city. As the word spread that the capital had been liberated, millions of people took to the streets, dancing, screaming, celebrating. Strangers hugged strangers. Champagne was being drunk straight from the bottle and sprayed in all directions. The war wasn't over yet, but Paris was free.

A very young woman in a bright yellow dress clambered up onto the Sherman's running board, threw her arms around Jacob, and began kissing his face, until he was polka-dotted with lipstick. She was raucously cheered on by Jacob's platoon-mates. Beau laughed so hard that he almost fell off the tank, to be crushed under the heavy tracks—not that the tank was moving very much. It was impossible to advance any faster than inch by inch through the rampaging mob.

The woman in yellow jumped back down to rejoin the revelers, still blowing kisses to Jacob and Bravo Company.

"What's the matter with you, High School?" Beau jeered. "Didn't you learn hand-to-hand combat at Fort Benning?"

Embarrassed, Jacob tried to wipe the lipstick off his cheeks, and only succeeded in smearing it even further.

"Get out of the road!" Lieutenant Hollister, the tank commander, bellowed into the crowd. "This is for your own safety!"

"Don't think they understand English, Lieutenant!" Leland called up to him.

"No, that's not it!" Jacob hollered. "They just don't care!"

That was closer to the truth. Nothing was going to spoil this celebration for the citizens of Paris. Everywhere, wine flowed, music played, and flowers were flung at tanks, jeeps, and half-tracks. Kisses rained down on soldiers. The French national anthem, "La Marseillaise," blared from fifteen places at once. During the long occupation, it had been forbidden.

On the opposite side of the broad avenue, a line of Nazi prisoners was being loaded onto a French army truck. Suddenly, the emotions of the crowd turned from celebration to hostility. The captured Germans were punched, kicked, and pelted with rocks. Their only protection came from the French Forces of the Interior—Resistance militiamen who had very little interest in being protectors to the hated Boches.

Suddenly, machine-gun fire erupted in the street. Three bullets ricocheted off the armor of the Sherman, dangerously close to Jacob's legs. The revelers scattered in an instant, scampering for cover in shops and cafés. Jacob and his platoon-mates came down off the tanks combat-ready, scanning the surrounding buildings for the source of the sniper. Despite the surrender, it was known that there were still pockets of enemies around the city, and in places, the fighting could be fierce. Bravo Company had hoped to avoid this. Yet here they were in the thick of it.

Another burst of gunfire tore into the road, sending fragments of pavement and cobblestone flying in all directions. A chip bounced off Jacob's helmet with a clang that rattled his brain a little.

The next thing he felt was 210 pounds of Beau Howell landing directly on top of him.

"High School—you hit?"

"No, I'm squashed!" Jacob shouted back. "Get off me!"

Beau rolled away and the two of them scrambled to get behind the tank. Bullets continued to keep them pinned down. Even the German prisoners were hiding under the truck that had been sent to take them into captivity.

"Where's it coming from?" Beau asked Leland.

"One of the buildings across the street," Leland replied. "But it could be any of them."

Warily, Jacob peered out from behind the Sherman's armored flank. Leland was right. The sniper could have been anywhere, lurking behind dozens of identical windows.

Then he saw it—a tiny hint of movement beside a chimney on one of the rooftops.

"Got him," he murmured, sighting along the barrel of his rifle. His finger tensed on the trigger, ready to shoot.

A tremendous boom rang out far louder than any rifle report. Still locked on his target, Jacob watched as a tank shell slammed into the building across the street. The roof and half the building disappeared in a cloud of smoke and dust. The machine-gun fire ceased.

On the Sherman, the hatch opened and Lieutenant

Hollister poked his head out of the turret to examine his handiwork.

It took both Beau and Leland to restrain Jacob from climbing the armored vehicle to throttle the tank commander. "What did you do that for?"

"I got him, didn't I?" Hollister asked mildly.

"I had him in my sights!" Jacob raved. "You didn't have to blow up the whole building! There could be people in there!"

Hollister shrugged. "You should have said something."

He signaled down to his driver. The Sherman roared back to life and began to rumble along the boulevard. Jacob's platoon-mates rushed to jump aboard.

Jacob wanted nothing to do with Hollister or his tank. Sullenly, he marched along behind it.

Beau reached out a hand. "Hop on, High School."

"I'll walk," Jacob seethed.

The big Texan laughed. "Don't be stubborn. It won't fix the top of that building if you get flat feet."

Jacob couldn't explain, even to himself, why the destruction of the building bothered him so much. The cities and towns of Normandy had been leveled to the ground; Saint-Lô was a smoldering ruin. Why did the damage done to this one row house in Paris—which was in great shape compared with those other places—bother him so much?

Because it hadn't been necessary. Jacob had been fighting for so long that the devastation was starting to feel normal. It had taken this building to remind him how awful all this really was.

The plume of smoke still hovered over the block when the

revelers returned to the street, dancing, singing, and celebrating. Hollister's tank slowed down again and progress was back to almost zero. Within a few minutes, the boulevard was just as mobbed as it had been before the incident.

As the only US service member within reach, Jacob was being thanked, kissed, hugged, slapped on the back, and loaded down with gifts of flowers and food. When an old woman tried to press a live chicken into his arms, he decided it was time to get back on the tank. Beau and Leland hoisted him aboard.

Beau grinned. "Get used to it, High School. This is what victory is like."

"You've got feathers on your grenade belt," Leland added.

Jacob brushed the feathers away, his expression grim. *Victory.* He was thinking of Freddie and all the other members of their unit who weren't here to see it.

Bravo Company spent three days in Paris. Most of the time, they were assigned to the Comédie-Française—one of the largest theaters in the city. There were no productions going on now. The place was a triage center for the wounded.

On the first day, some Canadian medics brought in an old woman who had been pulled from a collapsed building.

"Which one?" Jacob asked. "Was it the one we blew up? On that wide boulevard? You could see the Eiffel Tower in the distance?"

But Jacob had no French and the woman had no English,

so he never found out. The Canadians transferred her to a hospital a few hours later.

Another thing about Paris: There were soldiers from all the different Allied countries around—Americans, British, Canadians, French, and even some Polish units. They had been fighting on the same side since Normandy, but this was their first real chance to intermingle. Official policy was to let the French forces take the lead, since this was their capital.

The city was still a very strange place. Parisians insisted on celebrating the surrender of the German garrison even as rogue Nazi units continued to fight. It was as if someone was throwing a gigantic party in an active war zone.

On the fourth day, with no warning, Bravo Company was roused before dawn, loaded into trucks, and driven out of the city in a northeasterly direction.

"Where to, Lieutenant?" Beau asked McCoy.

The platoon leader made a face at him. "Where did you guys get the idea that they tell me any more than they tell you? You think Eisenhower talks it over with Bradley, and I'm next?"

"You should write your congressman," Jacob deadpanned.

"Smart aleck," McCoy snorted. "The Germans are falling back all over France. We're expecting counterattacks, but we don't know where. Battalion says be ready for anything."

"Lucky us," Beau groaned.

Progress was steady. For the first day, they could hear bombs and artillery all around them, but they themselves encountered no fighting. The next morning, their camp was strafed by two

German Messerschmitts. Jacob, Beau, and Leland spent a tense twenty minutes lying in the muddy earth under a jeep, praying that a direct hit wouldn't explode its gas tank. Miraculously, there were no casualties, although Sergeant Rajinsky knocked himself unconscious on a tree branch while running for cover.

As a medic was bandaging Rajinsky's head after the strafing, Captain Marone roared up in a jeep, his face all urgency. "New orders!" he barked at McCoy. "We're moving out!"

"Break camp!" McCoy bawled to the members of Third Platoon. To the company commander, he added, "Where to, Captain?"

"Retreating Germans are blowing every bridge in France," Marone explained. "But spotter planes found one they haven't gotten to yet—over the Aisne River." It came out *Aiz-nee*.

"I think it's pronounced *En*," Jacob volunteered helpfully.

The captain glared at him. "I don't care if it's pronounced *Harold*. Our orders are to take it and hold it before the enemy blows it up." He drove off.

Throwing their gear into the truck, Leland asked Jacob, "How come you know that? You don't speak French."

Jacob shrugged. "Geography class. I'm in high school, remember?"

Beau laughed. "Yeah, well, if you don't want to dig a lot of latrines, try not to dazzle the captain with your brilliance. Especially not in front of the whole platoon."

They were loaded up and on the move in a matter of minutes. Even if they hadn't heard their mission from Captain

Marone, Jacob would have been able to tell that they were in a big hurry. The trucks were driving far too fast for the French rural roads, which had been made even rougher by shell craters and battle debris. The trip was a teeth-rattling experience.

"Never thought I'd get a rougher ride than on the Higgins boat on D-Day," Leland complained, his face positively green. "But I guess that guy Higgins invented a truck too."

"It's like the bumper cars at the county fair," Beau put in morosely. "The only thing missing is cotton candy."

But no carnival ride lasted two hours without a break and included the prospect of enemy soldiers shooting at you at the end. They passed several French villages, some of them completely destroyed, others totally intact. It made Jacob reflect on the randomness of this war, where the difference between life and death was a roll of fate's dice.

As the journey went on, a familiar tension rose in the men of Bravo Company, edging out every other emotion, even the discomfort of motion sickness. They were all battle-hardened now, with a sixth sense for when trouble was coming.

Yet when the trucks came within sight of the Aisne and slowed to a cautious approach, there were no enemies in sight. Jacob stood up for a better view. A truss bridge about forty meters long spanned the river, its superstructure formed by a triangular lattice of steel beams. The spotter planes were right: It was intact. Up until this moment, it had been in Nazi hands. But as far as Bravo Company could see, there was no sign of an occupying force—no German soldiers, no tanks or staff cars, no Nazi flags.

The idling truck engines swelled to a crescendo and the

convoy moved forward toward the bridge. That was when Jacob's sharp eyes spied what the spotter planes had missed—tightly packed bundles strapped to the underside of the roadbed all across the span. There were at least five.

"Stop the trucks!" he bellowed, waving wildly at McCoy.

The lieutenant radioed Marone and Bravo Company came to a halt once again so Jacob's discovery could be investigated. Sure enough, the bundles turned out to be charges of dynamite strategically placed beneath the bridge.

"So the Germans were planning to blow this one too," Marone mused.

"Why didn't they?" McCoy wondered. "It's all ready to go."

There were two possibilities: 1) In the chaos of withdrawal, the bridge had been forgotten. Somewhere in the woods on the other side was a plunger with no German to plunge it. Or 2) The enemy had left a rear guard with orders to set off the dynamite when an Allied convoy was crossing.

Marone got in touch with battalion and explained the dilemma. Bravo Company sweated, waiting for an answer—ten minutes, fifteen, twenty. It wasn't hours, but in a time pressure situation, in a place where they could find themselves under sudden enemy fire at any second, it felt like forever. When the answer finally came, they understood the delay. Their situation had been passed all the way up the chain of command to SHAEF—Supreme Headquarters Allied Expeditionary Force. The order was from General Bradley himself: Remove the charges and take control of the bridge.

The army had engineers and sappers who were experts in

dealing with explosives. The problem was that the nearest of them was at least half a day away. The men of Bravo Company were going to have to take care of it themselves.

"All right," McCoy addressed his platoon. "Who's got some experience with dynamite?"

The silence was deafening.

Jacob raised a hand. "Back home, I helped the fire department set up the skyrockets for the Fourth of July."

"Shut up, High School!" Beau slammed an elbow into his ribs. To McCoy he said, "Don't listen to him, Lieutenant! He's stupid!"

McCoy ignored him and focused on Jacob. "What about it, Firestone? Think you can handle this?"

"I'll give it a try," Jacob agreed. "Somebody's got to do it. It might as well be me."

"Idiot!" Beau raged. "This isn't something you just 'give a try'! If it doesn't work out, they'll hear the explosion back in Paris! They'll be scraping bits of you off the Eiffel Tower—and bits of *me* too, because now I have to volunteer with you!"

Twenty minutes later, Jacob was swaying at the end of a makeshift rope harness, examining the suspicious package strapped to the underside of the bridge.

"What do you see, Firestone?" Marone called down to him.

"Looks like about a dozen bundles of dynamite, six sticks each," Jacob reported. "There are three different wires, red, black, and green . . ."

As Jacob went on, Captain Marone repeated the description into a shortwave radio. On the other end was a demolition expert attached to a unit of engineers. Speaking through the captain, the sapper asked Jacob several questions that Jacob answered to the best of his ability. The expert's final instructions were: Cut the red wire first, followed by the green wire. And if you were still alive, the black.

"Still alive?" Beau was horrified. "What's that supposed to mean? Doesn't he know for sure?"

There was still no sign of enemy presence on the other side. His hand shaking, Jacob took a pair of wire cutters and positioned the pincers around the red wire. It was hard to see what he was doing, because beads of perspiration were trickling down from his brow and stinging his eyes.

The men looking down at him from the bridge were just as tense. "Don't let the blades touch the metal contacts," Marone advised. "That could set off the whole charge."

"What?" came Beau's outraged voice. "Why didn't you tell him that first?"

"Get that man off my bridge," Marone ordered.

As Beau was marched ashore, Jacob remembered his friend's words: *Don't listen to him, Lieutenant. He's stupid.*

He was right, Jacob reflected. *I am stupid.* And he cut the red wire.

He waited to be consumed in a fireball. And when it didn't happen, he was so overjoyed that he snipped the green and then the black in rapid succession.

There was cheering from above. Emboldened, Jacob undid the strapping and watched as the deadly charge dropped into the river and disappeared harmlessly below the surface. He was hauled back up to the bridge, where he and three others were ordered to take out the remaining four charges.

Soon Jacob was hanging from his harness near the opposite terminus of the bridge. Now that he was an experienced bomb defuser, it was easy enough for him to snip the wires in order— red, green, black. He flashed a thumbs-up to the others to show he was done.

As he moved to unstrap his deactivated charge, his peripheral vision caught sight of just a hint of movement in the woods—the unmistakable squarish shape of a German army helmet.

"Look out!" he bellowed. But even as the warning was torn from him, he understood how completely useless it was. Trapped in their harnesses, the four GIs were dangling like worms on hooks. There was no escape.

With a deafening roar, the center charge detonated, turning the air red with flame. Suddenly, Leland was gone, and the bridge, in slow motion, was cracking open.

"Leland!" Jacob cried, oblivious to the hot shower of concrete and twisted metal blasting over him.

But there was no point in looking for his friend. So close to the explosion, there was zero chance Leland could have survived. Trembling with shock and weeping with grief, Jacob barely noticed he was falling—and that pieces of the roadway were raining down on him. He wriggled out of his harness and dropped to the river. A split second later a large chunk of the bridge, with the ropes still attached, splashed into the water mere inches away.

The plunge drove him under, and when he surfaced again,

coughing and spitting, the war had returned to this corner of France. A small platoon of Germans had appeared at the edge of the woods, firing on Bravo Company across the Aisne and at the hapless swimmers in the water. Jacob swam for the opposite shore, but the current drove him backward. He fought it, stroking with all his might, but every time he checked, his people seemed a little more distant. He was only ten meters from the far bank now, in the shadow of what used to be the bridge. It was nothing but a twisted ramp that led to thin air.

In a snap decision, he turned around and made for the closer bank. He came ashore perhaps fifteen meters downstream from the Germans, who were setting up a mortar to fire on the trucks across the river.

He splashed up on the bank, shocked and exhausted, but driven by a primitive impulse for survival. A quick glance confirmed that the Germans hadn't seen him yet. All their attention was concentrated on the river and the Allied forces on the other side. Jacob had no weapon except for his combat knife. He had taken off his rifle, ammunition belt, grenades, and pack when he'd climbed down from the bridge. All alone on the wrong side of the Aisne, he couldn't fight. His only option was escape.

Keeping low, he ran for the cover of the trees. He was almost there when a gunshot rang out and a bullet took a bite out of a white birch right by his head. He'd been spotted.

The thought gave his feet wings. He sprinted through the woods, dodging trees and underbrush. Wild thoughts flashed through his mind: What should he do? Hide? Climb a tree? He couldn't imagine either of those possibilities resulting in anything other than capture. Continuing to run seemed like the only option. But wasn't that taking him ever farther into enemy territory?

He burst into a clearing and looked around desperately. Pup tents circled a firepit. In dismay, he realized that he'd delivered himself to the German camp. There was only one soldier present, and he was burdened with an armload of firewood. The man gawked at the American suddenly in his presence. The wood dropped to the ground and the German lunged for a pistol that sat in front of one of the tents. Jacob got there before him and kicked the weapon into some tall grass.

What now? Jacob thought. Would he have to wrestle this enemy hand to hand? No—he could hear signs of pursuit behind him. He had to get away.

That was when he saw it—a motorcycle parked at the edge of the clearing. He made for it, moving like lightning. He jumped aboard, landing on the kick start, and the machine roared to life.

Jacob had only ridden a motorcycle once before—and it had terrified him. He had made one circle around a cul-de-sac and that had been more than enough. Now he was comparing terrors. This was definitely the lesser one.

He wasn't even sure German motorcycles operated the same way as their American counterparts. There was only one way to find out.

He twisted the throttle. The machine roared and leaped forward with such a burst of speed that it bucked him like a bronco. He picked himself off the ground and caught up with it about fifteen feet away, lying on its side, wheels still spinning. Using what little strength he had left, he hauled it upright, hopped back on, and took off, accelerating more slowly this time.

Hands shaking, he weaved between trees, aching for speed, but not daring to use it. Eventually, the bike's front wheel found a groove of hard-packed mud, and eventually thumped onto pavement, where it nearly rear-ended a German troop truck parked by the side of the road. He dismounted again, just long enough to plunge his knife into all four tires. He couldn't stop the enemy from coming after him, but that didn't mean he had to make it easy for them.

Instinct told him he had to get back to Bravo Company. But there was the little matter of a giant bridge that was no longer there. He was trapped—trapped on the wrong side of the Aisne.

It was a problem with no solution, a jigsaw puzzle with no pieces to fill in the holes. The closest thing to a plan Jacob could think of was to go the other way. Maybe he could somehow find another road that led to another bridge—one that hadn't been blown up yet, or one that had been repaired. The chances were slim to none, but he had to try.

He wheeled around and took off, speeding deeper toward who knew what. He felt his US Army uniform flashing on and off like a neon sign in the shape of a bull's-eye. If he ran into a German convoy, he was done for. But for now, he was still alive and still free. He twisted the throttle a little harder and the bike accelerated.

He risked a glance over his shoulder to see if he was being chased and almost lost control of the motorcycle. Riding the thing required 100 percent concentration. He could do it, but the slightest wriggle, the barest yawn, the merest blink would put him in the ditch. This powerful machine was his salvation for the moment, but it could be just as deadly as the enemy if he let it get away from him at this speed.

Eventually, he started to get the hang of the bike, leaning into the turns and squinting to protect his eyes from the onslaught of wind. Another advantage of being exposed to the elements: In no time, his soaked uniform was completely dry, and he'd stopped shivering with cold. He kept his eyes peeled for road signs—he remembered from Paris that *pont* meant *bridge*.

He shook his head to clear it. He was in big trouble that was getting bigger by the minute. But when he tried to think, the only subject that would come to his mind was poor Leland. There had been a dozen other guys on that bridge, but at least *they* had a chance.

First Freddie, now Leland. Oh, sure, their battalion alone had lost over a hundred men since D-Day, but of the four friends from Fort Benning, two were already gone. And here was Jacob, trapped behind enemy lines, in grave danger of becoming number three. At least Beau's big mouth had gotten him kicked off the bridge, so that meant he was relatively safe.

A loud horn jarred Jacob out of his reverie. Lost in his mourning, he'd been sailing down the middle of the road, directly in the path of an oncoming car. Jacob swerved to the side, peering in through the windshield to see if the driver wore a German uniform.

This turned out to be a mistake. His front tire hit a pothole and the handlebars were wrenched from his nerveless fingers. By the time he regained his grip, it was too late. The motorcycle was airborne and so was Jacob.

They parted company somewhere near the apex of the jump. He came down in the ditch with a force that turned the whole world black. He never heard the motorcycle hit the ground a few feet away from him.

How long did he lie there unconscious? He had no way of knowing. Was it dark now? Or was his vision clouded by his injury? He knew he was injured. That much pain had to mean something.

No, it was a shadow—a face leaning over him.

"American?" a deep voice asked.

Jacob looked up, blinking, struggling to focus. The man wore no uniform, but that didn't mean he wasn't the enemy. Captain Marone had told them of SS officers who wore civilian clothes.

In answer, Jacob fumbled his dog tags from under his collar and began reading his serial number. That and his name and rank were all he was required to give.

The man held out a hand. "You are a long way from Broadway, monsieur."

Jacob's eyes fixed on the stranger's reaching hand. He wore a ring engraved with a symbol Jacob had never seen before—a double-barred cross.

It was the last thing he would see for three days.

CHAPTER TWENTY-TWO

OUTSIDE SOISSONS, FRANCE—
MAY 3

"It looked bigger the last time I was here." G.G.'s voice had a tone of complaint to it. "And the drop down to the water was definitely farther."

The Citroën was parked at the side of the road, and the three Firestones gazed out at the span over the Aisne River.

"Don't forget, G.G.," Trevor pointed out. "It's not the same bridge. They had to rebuild it, remember?"

"I'm not likely to forget," the old soldier growled. "It was a pile of broken Tinkertoys the last time I saw it." He stepped out onto the span and began to walk across, limping a little from the shrapnel lodged in his hip.

"Grandpa," Dad said tentatively, "it's windy out over the water. Maybe we should take the car."

G.G. glared at him. "What am I, a delicate flower? They blew this bridge out from under me, and I'm still here. I don't think a little wind is going to kill me."

Trevor and his father exchanged a look. Ever since they'd arrived in Paris, G.G. had become increasingly irritable. He had always been a crusty character, but lately, he was downright hard to get along with, snapping at his grandson and great-grandson.

"Don't take it personally, Trev," Dad soothed. "G.G. loves you more than anything. But I think this trip down memory lane is harder on him than he expected it to be. It's like the closer we get to Sainte-Régine, the weirder he gets."

"Of course he's weird," Trevor told his father. "This is where Leland died."

The old man had stopped in the center of the bridge and was peering over the side, his knuckles white as he gripped the railing. A passing car slowed and the driver rolled down the window.

"Monsieur?"

"I'm not jumping, if that's what you're worried about," G.G. snapped. "Been there, done that."

The car drove past and the old soldier returned his attention to the Aisne. "Red, then green, then black," he said quietly.

"What's he talking about?" Dad whispered as they started out toward him.

"Disarming the charges," Trevor explained. "First you cut the red wire; then the green; and if you're still alive, the black. Weren't you paying attention when he told us the story?"

"I'm older than you, so I've heard a lot more of his stories," Dad explained. "After a while, they all run together, and the only thing I remember about war is I want no part of it. It breaks things and people. Like this bridge—and Leland."

When Trevor started ahead, his father held him back. "Maybe it's a good idea to give your great-grandfather a little more time alone with his thoughts."

They watched G.G. at the rail, gazing out at the river. Trevor could only imagine what must be whirling through the old soldier's mind at a moment like this. Maybe he was remembering the explosion or his wild drop into the water. Maybe he was saying goodbye to his friend Leland one last time.

And then G.G. looked up. "Well, what are you two waiting for? I don't have all day." And he continued to march across the bridge.

Trevor ran ahead to catch up with the old man, while Dad went back for the car. On the other side, G.G. went looking for the clearing where the Nazi encampment had been.

"Where you kicked the gun away from the guy with the firewood!" Trevor enthused.

"Stupid forest," G.G. complained. "Maybe it was farther upstream."

Dad parked the car on this side of the bridge and joined the search. "Or maybe the clearing isn't there anymore," he put in. "Seventy-five years is more than enough time for little bushes to become tall trees."

It seemed to bother the old man. "Nothing's the same. The road's different too—wider, smoother. I don't know how I rode that motorcycle on it the way it used to be."

"You have to finish telling us the story," Trevor urged. "Trapped behind enemy lines, with no bridge to get back to your unit. What happened? Did you have to kill anybody?"

"Are you kidding? I darn near got killed myself. I was going like sixty when I went into the ditch. And when I came to, I looked up and saw . . ."

"Saw what?" Trevor prompted breathlessly.

A shudder ran through the old man's long, lean frame. His shaking hands latched onto the trunk of the tree in front of him. If it hadn't been for that, he might have fallen to the ground.

"Grandpa!" Dad jumped forward to support his unsteady grandfather.

He and Trevor managed to guide G.G. over to the car and sit him down on the hood. Trevor popped open a water bottle and the old man sipped from it.

"It's no big deal," G.G. insisted. "I was just a little dizzy for a minute."

"For a man your age, being 'a little dizzy' *is* a big deal," Dad insisted.

"Don't be ridiculous. I'm fine."

"I want to hear that from somebody who *knows*," Dad decided. "We're going to find a doctor."

G.G. turned blazing eyes on Trevor. "Talk some sense into your father."

Trevor gulped. "This time he's right."

🎖 🎖 🎖 🎖

The nearest doctor turned out to be in Soissons, a small city about the same size as Saint-Lô. That was where the similarity ended, though. While Saint-Lô had been almost entirely rebuilt after the war, Soissons was an ancient town, with some buildings dating back as far as Roman times.

Dr. Duceppe spent about twenty minutes examining his elderly American patient. He pronounced Mr. Firestone Senior in excellent health for a man his age. "He is simply tired. It is exhausting, this tourism. Sometimes, we need vacations from our vacations, *n'est-ce pas*?"

"It's not a vacation," the old man told him. "We're going to Sainte-Régine."

"G.G.'s getting a medal," Trevor supplied. "He liberated the town during the war."

The doctor smiled tolerantly. "Sainte-Régine has been there for hundreds of years. Another twenty-four hours and it will still be in the same place. A fine dinner, a relaxing evening, and a good night's sleep will make all the difference for your war hero. That is my prescription."

All three Firestones thought that sounded like a pretty sensible idea. In the waiting room, Dad emailed their hosts in Sainte-Régine that they would be delayed by a day.

As they left the hospital, none of them noticed the boy and girl seated on their motorcycle parked halfway down the block.

🤺 🤺 🤺 🤺

"He eats too much, this old man," Philippe Lafleur commented sourly.

The two cousins watched from a park bench concealed by

154

bushes. Across the boulevard, the Firestones were enjoying a fancy dinner on the outdoor patio of their hotel restaurant.

Juliette's thoughts were elsewhere. "But what are they doing here in Soissons?"

"Living like kings," her older cousin said bitterly. "While we sleep in hostels, battling cockroaches, the Americans stay in the finest hotels."

"You're not listening," Juliette insisted. "The boy—Trevor—posted their whole itinerary on his Instagram. They were in Normandy because the old man landed on the beach there. They were in the hedgerows, where he fought. And Saint-Lô. And in Paris because he was there for the liberation."

Philippe was impatient. "So?"

"So he never went to Soissons as a soldier, and it wasn't on the Instagram list. Their schedule has them in Sainte-Régine tonight. Why are they here and not there?"

Philippe looked hopeful. "Are you saying that we have succeeded in scaring them off? That they came to Soissons instead of Sainte-Régine? And from here they will go home?"

She shook her head. "Not very likely. Since Normandy, we've been harassing them, yet still they came. They are stubborn."

"So why this diversion to Soissons?" Philippe asked.

"Perhaps it is exactly what it appears to be," she mused. "They needed a doctor, probably for the old monster. At such an age, ailments are many."

Her cousin was skeptical. "Whatever his ailment, it has not

affected his appetite. Is that a second piece of pie? I hope he chokes on it!"

Juliette frowned across the boulevard at the dining trio. "He doesn't look like a monster," she commented, half to herself.

"And you come to this conclusion how?" Philippe challenged. "This is no case of mistaken identity. Is he not Private Jacob Firestone, United States Army, the man who destroyed our family?"

She sighed. "I suppose so. But they seem like such a nice family—especially how the old man interacts with the boy."

Philippe scowled. "I remind you that he's the reason *we* have no older generation to interact with. If he still intends to go to Sainte-Régine, we will make him pay."

Juliette couldn't argue with him. She'd heard the story, passed down from generation to generation. It was impossible to get it wrong, because their family was so small. And there was only one villain, one name to remember: Jacob Firestone.

Now Sainte-Régine wanted to celebrate this man as a hero.

Not if the Lafleur family had anything to say about it.

The two cousins watched as the Firestones paid their bill and disappeared into the hotel lobby. The old man didn't seem all that sick, she reflected, but it was possible that he'd slowed down a little since their arrival in France. She remembered him striding vigorously off the ferry in Cherbourg, showing all the arrogance of the young soldier he had been in 1944. What did the Americans call it—attitude? Some of that was missing in him tonight. And was that a slight limp?

"Let's go back," Philippe decided. "They will be up early, those three. And if they head to Sainte-Régine, we should be close behind them."

That was another thing about the Americans: They awoke at the crack of dawn, eager to start their day. It was so uncivilized.

"You go ahead," Juliette told him. "I'll walk. It's not far."

With a shrug, her cousin climbed onto the motorcycle, donned his helmet, and putt-putted away.

Through a large picture window, Juliette could still see the Firestones in the lobby, waiting for the elevator. Was it wishful thinking on her part that they seemed so harmless, so *ordinary*? This was the hated Jacob Firestone. She watched Trevor veer away from the adults, lost in the depths of his phone screen. He could have been any one of her school friends from Sainte-Régine.

He stepped back out to the patio, phone held high, searching for a signal. And the next thing she knew, his eyes were off the phone and locked onto her.

She leaped to her feet. Her first impulse was to run, as she had done before. But something kept her there as the American crossed the boulevard and approached her.

He said the last thing she expected. "Hi."

"*Bonjour,*" she replied warily.

"I know you, right? You've been following us since Omaha Beach."

Juliette didn't answer. She just stood, letting the emotions swirl inside of her. For the first time since the war, a Lafleur stood opposite a hated Firestone.

He grew angry at her silence. "Have you been messing with our car? I don't care about the dead bird, but slashing the tires—that's not right. What did we ever do to you?"

Juliette felt a long, bitter speech forming in her mind, one she was determined would never come out her mouth. She and Philippe could get in big trouble for what they'd done. *Admit nothing!* she ordered herself.

"The doctor says my great-grandfather is overtired," Trevor persisted. "Well, maybe he wouldn't be if we didn't have to waste a day waiting for new tires. And all he's trying to do is go back to the town he liberated seventy-five years ago. He's a hero!"

Juliette's eyebrows shot up. "A hero? Is that what they told you?"

"Nobody had to tell me anything," Trevor snapped back. "It's in the history books."

Her eyes sprayed sparks, and it almost erupted from her— the entire horrible story. But instead, she spat, "There is much that your American history books leave out!"

She spun on her heel and stormed away into the night.

CHAPTER TWENTY—THREE

OUTSIDE SAINTE—RÉGINE, FRANCE— SEPTEMBER 2, 1944

When Jacob's vision finally returned to him, he found himself lying on a sweet-smelling hay-filled mattress. He blinked, trying to bring everything into focus. This wasn't home. This wasn't the army. He found himself staring at a dappled wall of beige masonry with white dots. He reached out to touch it and instantly recognized the oblong item that came away in his hand.

"Potatoes?"

"Pommes de terre," corrected a voice behind him. "Welcome back, monsieur."

Jacob wheeled on the mattress. He knew that face. Memories flooded in on him—the bridge gone, Leland disappearing in a burst of flame, a wild motorcycle ride through enemy territory—

"Where am I?" Jacob demanded. "Who are you? Why are you holding me here?"

"Calm down, monsieur," the man told him. "We are not the Boches—the Germans. You are with the Free French—La Résistance. René Lafleur, at your service."

Jacob scrambled up. "I have to get back to my unit!"

René took hold of his shoulders and eased him back into bed. "In time. First you must recover."

Jacob was about to protest, but he realized that the Frenchman was right. It hadn't taken much for René to force him back onto his pillow. Jacob accepted the fact that he wasn't strong enough to be any use to Bravo Company. His ribs were so sore that a deep breath was practically unbearable. He was almost panting just to avoid that pain. Also, his head hurt, and there was a buzzing in his ears that reminded him of being menaced by a single mosquito.

"What is this place?" he asked, and was alarmed at how feeble his voice sounded.

René smiled. "You are missing your American wall-to-wall carpeting and feather bed? I apologize that my root cellar is not more elegant, but it is safe from the prying eyes of the Boches. We are occupied, yes?"

"I didn't mean it that way," Jacob stammered. "I'm grateful."

"Wait until you taste my wife's cooking before you express your gratitude," René advised him. "She is a good woman, but should not be allowed anywhere near a kitchen."

A snicker was torn from Jacob, even though he didn't feel much like laughing. Not with Leland gone and Bravo Company who knew where.

"You will see," René promised.

In all, Jacob spent eight days recovering in the secret cellar of René's farmhouse, outside the town of Sainte-Régine. He soon learned that the cellar was far more than a place to store potatoes and turnips; it was a local headquarters for Resistance members from all around this part of France. Nor was Jacob the first Allied service member to enjoy the hospitality of the Lafleur farmhouse. René was part of a network that helped smuggle downed pilots back to England via Spain. More than twenty had slept on that very mattress and experienced Madame's notorious cooking.

Jacob had to admit that even the US Army served better food than Madame Lafleur. Her saving grace turned out to be that she was the nicest person he'd ever met. There seemed to be no end to her kindness, and that was something a soldier received very little of. Madame understood what the consequences would be if the Germans found an American infantryman hidden in her home. Sometimes she was even called upon to entertain and feed German officers who were in the district. When that happened, tension crackled throughout the wood-frame house, especially in the cellar, where Jacob didn't dare move a muscle. He would become a prisoner of war, which would be bad enough. But French citizens who were discovered to be members of the Resistance were shot on the spot.

Usually, Jacob wasn't alone in the cellar. The five Lafleur children were always around, bringing him food and basins of hot water for washing. And there were Resistance fighters— grim-faced men and women in dark clothing who came at all hours of the night and spoke in low voices. Jacob was not able to understand their conversations, but there was no mistaking the seriousness of what they were involved in. They were kind to an American soldier, but wary too. They placed their hopes for liberation with the Allies, yet distrusted them too. There were spies everywhere.

As Jacob's bruised ribs healed and his headaches receded, he began to ask René when he'd be able to rejoin his unit.

"You feel fine because you are lying on your back doing nothing," the Frenchman explained. "Being a soldier takes much more than that."

"But I'm useless here," Jacob insisted. "Worse than that, I'm a danger to your family."

"You are a *blessing* to my family," René amended. "You give my children the opportunity to practice the English they learn in your American movies. And you complain about my wife's cooking slightly less than everybody else. Most important, you fight the Boches, and for this you must be completely healthy. I will tell you when it is time to leave."

Jacob had to be satisfied with that. But when René began making inquiries through the Resistance network as to the whereabouts of Bravo Company, Jacob knew the time would be soon.

"Tonight there will be no moon," René told him one morning.

The message was clear: He was leaving.

They waited until one a.m. Jacob passed from bed to bed, whispering his farewells to the children. When he hugged

Madame, it was almost as hard as parting from his own mother.

"Hurry up," mumbled René. "You are lucky she didn't poison you."

Madame just laughed. "Come back to us, *cher* Jacob. Bring your General Eisenhower and chase these Boches away."

"I'll try," Jacob promised. Then he and René slipped out into the darkness.

They traveled on foot to avoid detection, staying away from roads. After two hours, they met up with another Resistance contact, who would be taking Jacob the rest of the way.

Jacob turned back to thank René, who had undoubtedly saved his life. The man was already gone, melted into the night. Jacob had spent barely a week with the Free French. Yet he was certain that, even if he lived to be a very old man, he would never see their like again.

"*Allons-y*," said the second Resistance man. *Let's go*.

Jacob was never aware of the moment he crossed into Allied-controlled territory. The boundary had been the Aisne before, but he noticed no river. That was the reality of this war. Battle lines changed by the day, the hour, and sometimes even the minute.

Eventually, they came to the top of a rise, and the guide pointed to the valley below. "*Voilà*," he said with satisfaction.

Jacob was mystified. "I don't see anything."

"Look carefully."

It took a few minutes for the outline of the encampment to reveal itself to Jacob's night sight. Slowly, the shapes of trucks and tents began to emerge out of the blackness.

He started down the hill, picking his way carefully,

working hard to make plenty of noise. The US Army could shoot an unidentified intruder just as easily as the Germans could—and you would be just as dead from a friendly bullet.

Yet the closer he got, the more he basked in the warmth of something very much like a homecoming. It took all his strength of will to keep himself from running.

When the flashlight beam fixed on him, he was blinded and frozen to the spot.

"It's me!" he exclaimed, raising his arms. "Jacob Firestone! Don't shoot!"

"Firestone?"

The sentry focused the light and squinted at Jacob. Jacob recognized Private Abilene.

"Put the gun down, Charlie, it's really me!" Jacob pleaded.

Before he knew it, Jacob was surrounded by jubilant sentries, laughing and pounding his back and shoulders.

"Welcome back, kid!"

"We thought you bought it at the bridge!"

"Where the heck have you been?"

"It's a long story," Jacob admitted. "I better save it for the captain."

As the sentries walked him into camp, he could hear his name passed from tent to tent by sleepy voices. Suddenly, he was knocked to the ground by a force the likes of which he hadn't experienced since the bridge blew up.

Shocked, he rolled over onto his back, struggling to recover. A white face hovered over him. Beau, roused from sleep and nearly beside himself.

"High School? That you?"

"It was before you crushed me!"

He was hauled to his feet and enfolded in a bear hug that went on a lot longer than he expected.

"We thought you were gone, High School." Beau's voice was hoarse and shaking with emotion. "Like the others. Like Leland."

It had been barely three months since D-Day. It felt like centuries.

CHAPTER TWENTY-FOUR

SAINTE-RÉGINE, FRANCE—MAY 5

"Still just one road going into Sainte-Régine, huh, G.G.?" Trevor asked as the Citroën labored up the incline, bounded by mature apple orchards on both sides.

"Same old two-lane nothing," the old soldier mumbled glumly. "Seventy-five years and they couldn't do any better than this."

The doctor may have said G.G. was fine, but Trevor knew it wasn't so. His great-grandfather just wasn't himself. The old soldier loved to talk—especially about his war experiences, and especially to Trevor, who was his most enthusiastic audience. Talking about Sainte-Régine should have brought out animated stories of massive artillery shells devastating a column of tanks, half-tracks, and troop carriers, the air thick with the aroma of gunpowder and shattered apples. Now they were in the *real place*, where Trevor could picture the rumbling Shermans rubbing up against the branches of the trees. And what did G.G. have to say about it? Practically nothing.

Dad had tried to explain it before they'd left Soissons that morning. "You have to understand, Trev—the closer we get to Sainte-Régine, the more real all this becomes for your great-grandfather."

"Real should be *good*," Trevor argued. "G.G. was a hero! This was the greatest part of his whole life!"

"He *was* a hero," Dad conceded. "But when it comes to war, real is never good. People were dying every day, all around him. Now, for the first time in decades, he's back in the place where it happened. And it's having an emotional effect on him. You can't take it personally if he's not as entertaining as you expect him to be. This isn't a YouTube video; it's his life. And all we can do is stand by him and support him."

Typical Dad, Trevor thought as they continued through the orchards. The whole world was saved from catastrophe, but he couldn't say anything positive because it was a war. And to him, war was bad, no matter what.

G.G. hadn't always been so down on this trip. Back at Fort Benning, in England, and in Normandy, the stories had been better than ever—vivid, exciting, even funny sometimes. But now, as they approached the place of his greatest triumph, he was glum, super quiet, crabby. Worse, he was like an old man. Sure, ninety-three *was* old. But G.G. didn't do any of the typical old-person things, like hobbling on a cane or never getting out of his chair. When he walked, he took long strides, moving with purpose, as if he had somewhere to go and he didn't want to waste time getting there. When he went to watch Trevor play soccer or baseball, he stalked up and down the sidelines, criticizing the refs, refusing to sit. He was more like a gray-haired kid. Not anymore. And since a doctor had just told them his health was excellent, Trevor had to ask himself the question: What was wrong?

He was determined to bring back the real G.G. When a gap in the orchard provided a view of the countryside, he asked, "Are we going to see René's farmhouse on the way into town?"

G.G. was tight-lipped as ever. "It isn't there anymore."

"How can you be sure?" Trevor persisted.

"Trev," Dad said warningly. "It's been seventy-five years. I'm sure a lot of things have changed around here. Right, Grandpa?"

The old soldier remained silent, staring out the window, his expression inscrutable.

At last, orchards gave way to houses, and they entered the town. Sainte-Régine was considerably smaller than Saint-Lô, but larger than some of the villages they'd passed through in the hedgerow country of Normandy. By far the largest building was the church, which was a gray stone structure, probably hundreds of years old. That meant it hadn't been destroyed during the battle.

Rubbernecking in the Citroën, Trevor was dying to ask about the big German gun that had rained shells down on the only approach to Sainte-Régine. Where had it been located? How had the American attackers managed to knock it out of commission? He sensed, though, that maybe Dad was right— now was not the time to question the old soldier. Maybe tomorrow, after the ceremony, when G.G. was sporting his new medal, he'd be in more of a World War II mood.

The finest hotel in Sainte-Régine, Au Toit Rouge, was near the center of town, in a commercial area of newer buildings. Growing up, Philippe and Juliette Lafleur had always been told that it was for wealthy visitors from Paris and other major European cities. The biggest treat Juliette could remember was being taken out to the Au Toit Rouge restaurant for her twelfth birthday.

Now the two cousins peered around the corner as the Citroën pulled up in front of the canopy and the hated American soldier Jacob Firestone stepped onto the red carpet. Alerted to the hero's arrival, the hotel manager rushed to greet him, bobbing and bowing and making a complete idiot out of himself.

"Excuse me while I throw up," Philippe snarled in disgust.

"So hard we tried to keep them away," Juliette said grimly as two uniformed bellhops unloaded the Firestones' luggage onto a cart and wheeled it inside. "At least we let them know that they are unwelcome here."

They watched as a porter presented G.G. with a gift basket of gleaming Sainte-Régine apples. A very young girl offered the three Americans flowers and curtsied like she was meeting royalty.

"Yes"—Philippe's voice dripped with sarcasm—"very unwelcome. It should be torches and pitchforks, not apples and flowers. Even worse, they'll be staying in the Ambassador Suite. The mayor himself arranged it."

"How do you know that?" Juliette asked.

"I have a friend who is one of those uniformed lackeys," Philippe replied. "Nothing but the best for our 'hero.'"

Juliette sighed. "At least it will be over soon. Tomorrow he will be honored as the savior of Sainte-Régine. It will be unpleasant for those of us who know the truth, but it will be temporary. Then he will take his medal and go home to America."

Philippe's face darkened. "He does not have his medal yet. And he never will—if we have anything to say about it."

She shook her head sadly. "It is too late. He is already here."

Philippe reached down and picked up a large piece of broken cobblestone. "Perhaps we have not yet been as persuasive as we might be."

Juliette watched as the elderly Jacob Firestone was helped inside the hotel entrance by his grandson on one side and great-grandson on the other. He looked tired and frail, his limp far more pronounced than before.

She turned on her cousin. "You're not seriously planning to attack a feeble old man."

"Think of the feeble old man you speak of," Philippe shot back. "We can ask our family how feeble he was when he did what he did. Wait—we cannot. Most of them are dead, thanks to *him*."

Juliette was torn. The villain of her entire life had been Jacob Firestone, the American soldier whose rash and dangerous actions had led to the extermination of the Lafleur clan. For generations, while other French families had flourished and multiplied, the Lafleurs had withered. Even now, three-quarters of a century later, she had one cousin of her generation.

One. She had only Philippe, and Philippe had only her.

But *this* Jacob Firestone—the one who had come to France this year—was a helpless old wreck of a man. She hadn't felt this way when the family had arrived on the ferry in Cherbourg. But now that she'd seen the American soldier up close—and met the great-grandson who loved him—she knew in her heart that revenge would not be sweet. What was past was past. A terrible thing had happened. It would not be remedied by another terrible thing, regardless of one man's guilt.

"Put that down before you drop it on your foot," she told Philippe.

Philippe set his jaw. "He needs to know that not everyone is happy to strew rose petals at his feet."

"He knows," she assured him. "That's why we created La Vérité. That's why we followed him and his family all across France. Put down the stone. It is done."

He glared at her, eyes burning. Then the tension disappeared between them and he let the rock drop. "You are probably right," he said. "We have already wasted too much of our lives on this old fool."

He turned on his heel and was gone.

Juliette continued to gaze at the entrance to the Au Toit Rouge, even though the Firestones were on their way up to their suite and out of view. She felt no sadness at calling an end to La Vérité—only relief. It made no sense to carry on a grudge that had been in existence for more than seventy-five years. It served no purpose, delivered no justice, brought no one back from the dead.

What was an enemy, after all? She thought back to her meeting with Trevor outside the restaurant in Soissons. A Lafleur and a Firestone, finally face-to-face. Was he a terrible person? Not at all. He was a boy about her age, not much different from her and everyone she went to school with. Sure, they'd argued a little. So what? Mostly, what she remembered about Trevor was his loyalty to his great-grandfather—his concern for the old man's health. Loyalty—that was a good quality. Something admirable.

Her thoughts were interrupted by the unmistakable crash of shattering glass. Alarmed, Juliette ran into the alley behind the hotel, toward the source of the noise.

The roar of an engine cut the air. Juliette barely had time to dive out of the way before Philippe swept by on his motorcycle, fleeing the scene. He wore his helmet and visor, but the stiffness of his jaw radiated grim determination.

She turned her gaze up at the rear of the hotel. A plate-glass window on the third floor had been smashed.

"What the—?" His photographs of the ride into Sainte-Régine only partially uploaded to Instagram, Trevor dropped his phone and dashed into the living room of the Ambassador Suite.

The floor-to-ceiling picture window was all but gone, its glittering shards on the carpet. The rock that did the deed sat in the middle of the pile of glass—a small piece of cobblestone from Sainte-Régine's streets. Dad and G.G. stood back from the opening, rigid with shock.

Trevor stepped forward and peered down to the alley. She was standing there—that girl—gazing up at him. Their eyes locked, and she shook her head vehemently, as if to deny responsibility for this act of violence.

Trevor's anger flared. Did she think he was stupid? She was standing *right there*!

"Trev!" Dad stepped forward, grabbed Trevor by the arm, and pulled him away from the broken window.

"But it's *her*!" Trevor protested. "That girl who's been chasing us since Omaha Beach! We have to call the police!"

He shook himself free and peered back down to the street. The girl was gone.

"It's okay, Trev," Dad tried to soothe.

"It's not okay!" Trevor snapped back. "We can't let her get away with this!"

Dad started for the phone. "I'll call the front desk. They'll find us another room."

"Another room?" Trevor echoed. "Is that all this means to you? We were just attacked!"

"We've been under attack since before we left Connecticut," G.G. mumbled.

Trevor stared at him. "What are you talking about?"

"You heard me," the old soldier confirmed. "There are people around here who never wanted me back in Sainte-Régine.

Your father didn't want to worry you about it, but we've been getting threats over that blasted Internet everyone thinks is so important."

Trevor wheeled back on his father. "Is that true?"

Dad nodded reluctantly. "It started with postings to the Sainte-Régine Facebook page. A group calling itself La Vérité, warning G.G. not to come. We figured it was just a couple of cranks. But incidents started happening. The dead bird on our windshield. The slashed tires. And then you started telling us about the blond girl."

"There's a guy too," Trevor supplied. "Older. They drive around on his motorcycle."

"We thought it would peter out," Dad went on. "Instead, it's getting worse. In Paris, we found something in our room that looked like a bomb. It wasn't. But whoever put it there wanted us to know that it could have been. I was ready to turn around and go home, but your grandfather wouldn't hear of it."

G.G.'s voice was quiet but firm. "I didn't let Hitler scare me off last time, and I'm not going to let a couple of punks chase me away now."

Trevor was stunned and a little hurt. Ever since the trip had begun, Dad had been keeping a secret from him. He felt Trevor wasn't mature enough to handle it—like he was two years old or something! It wasn't *Dad* who'd found the mysterious kids who were behind La Vérité. In Normandy, when Trevor had suspected they were being followed, Dad told him he was imagining things. How unfair was that? But then G.G. started getting weird and quiet, so everybody's focus changed to making sure the old man was okay.

Now here they were, in Sainte-Régine, the main destination of their journey, standing in a pile of broken glass in a ruined hotel suite. Trevor felt so many emotions at once: rage at the girl; anger at Dad; concern for G.G.; and fear that the next attack might come at the ceremony tomorrow and do them real harm.

Yet one question arose from the turmoil in his mind, pushing all other thoughts into the background:

"Why would anyone want to keep G.G. from coming back to Sainte-Régine?" Trevor demanded. "He helped liberate the whole town! He's a hero!"

G.G.'s face was gray. "Maybe I'm not the hero that people say I am—at least not to everybody."

Trevor looked bewildered. "What are you talking about? Of course you're a hero!"

Dad stepped in. "Why don't we call the desk and get our suite changed? I'm sure we'll all be a lot calmer when we can relax away from this mess."

The old soldier would not back down. "You're the one who's always complaining that the kid glamorizes war. He needs to hear this." He took a deep breath. "And it's time you heard it too."

CHAPTER TWENTY-FIVE

NEAR LAON, FRANCE— SEPTEMBER 10, 1944

Bravo Company had lost nine men on the bridge—Jacob had originally been listed as number ten. Luckily, he had returned before anyone had notified his family that he was missing in action. The thought of his parents having to endure that terrible visit from the Department of War was almost impossible for Jacob to bear. He ached for Freddie's family, who had already received that call, and for Leland's, who would very soon. These days, when a car full of somber-faced men in uniform parked on your street, you could only pray that they weren't coming to your door.

He had only been gone a little over a week, but Jacob found Bravo Company different. The soldiers were grimmer, quieter. There was less conversation and far fewer jokes. The men spent more time writing letters home. There were strangers, replacements—which only made Jacob think of the faces that were no longer there.

"Everything's changed," Beau tried to explain. "When we landed at Omaha, none of us expected to last five minutes, and we made our peace with that. We didn't worry, because there were so many ways to get killed that you couldn't keep them straight. But now that we've all made it this far, we're starting to think, hey, we might just live through this war. And the minute you've got that idea in your head, High School, you've got more worries than you know what to do with."

Another symptom of this: Everyone was suddenly interested in military strategy. Bitter stories abounded of vast forces sent to operations in Belgium and Holland while right here in France, undermanned, underequipped units were taking heavy casualties fighting from town to town.

As the men of Bravo Company rattled east in trucks, their column ground to a halt at a section of road that had been narrowed by a huge bomb crater. Bravo pulled over to the side to let another truck pass in the opposite direction.

At first, the westbound vehicle was greeted with jeers and catcalls.

"Turn around, dummies!" Beau shouted. "The fighting's behind you!"

"How about you get out of the way for us?" Jacob added.

But as soon as the truck pulled alongside them, the chorus of boos died out. The back was loaded with wounded, some in desperate condition, covered in white bandages soaked through with red blood. It was a grim reminder that the consequences of war were never far away.

"Where are you boys coming from?" Sergeant Rajinsky asked gently when the two vehicles were side by side.

Most of the wounded were too listless to reply. But one young soldier, wrapped in bandages like a mummy, managed to rasp, "Sainte-Régine."

Jacob jumped up. "What's happening in Sainte-Régine? There's fighting there?"

"It was supposed to be easy—only a small garrison defending the town." The youngster groaned. "They cut us to pieces. There's only one road in, and they've got a giant gun locked onto it. We never got within a klick."

"Calm down, son," Rajinsky soothed. "You boys are going to be just fine. They're going to take good care of you."

The truck of wounded eased past them, leaving Bravo Company silent and brooding.

Except Jacob. "I need to see the captain," he told Rajinsky urgently.

"And I need to see the president," Rajinsky retorted, "for an immediate discharge. The captain's a busy man, Firestone."

"He needs to hear this," Jacob insisted. "That town those guys got shot up in—Sainte-Régine. That's where I was."

The next time the convoy stopped to refuel, Jacob was hustled to Marone's jeep and presented to the captain.

"Make it quick, Firestone. We just got new orders."

"We're going to Sainte-Régine, aren't we, sir?" Jacob asked.

The captain's eyes narrowed. "How would you know that?"

"From the wounded they were evacuating past our convoy. That's our new mission, right? To reinforce that unit and take the town? I can help."

Lieutenant McCoy leaned into the conversation. "We weren't thinking of doing it without you, if that's what you're worried about."

"Hear me out," Jacob pleaded. "The farmhouse where they

nursed me back to health—that was outside Sainte-Régine."

The captain and the lieutenant exchanged a meaningful look. They had debriefed Jacob after his return from the farmhouse, so they knew about René Lafleur and his Resistance connection.

"Do you think you can reestablish contact with the Resistance?" Marone asked.

"I know I can. If there's a big gun hidden in Sainte-Régine that's making it impossible for us to attack, the Resistance will do everything they can to help us get rid of it. That's all they talked about—finding a way to help the Allies liberate their town."

Captain Marone thought it over for what seemed like a long time. Finally, he said, "Stick around, Firestone. We might actually be able to do some business here."

The moon was back, but just a sliver. Jacob was grateful to be able to see a little bit as he made his way cross-country through the orchards that surrounded Sainte-Régine. When he'd left the farmhouse, less than a week before, the night had been like black velvet.

As he moved, Captain Marone's ominous words echoed in his brain: "I can't order you to do this, Firestone. You're going to be behind enemy lines, meeting with people the Germans would shoot on sight. If you get caught, there's nothing we can do for you."

"I understand," Jacob had said.

Scrambling over roots and between trees, he realized that he *hadn't* understood at all. He had risked his life dozens of times as a member of Bravo Company—on Omaha Beach, in the hedgerows of Normandy, crossing France. But what was different now was the fact he was alone. Not just separated from his unit, but acting totally on his own.

When he reached the narrow road, he paused, taking stock. He and the two officers had spent hours poring over the area maps. Naturally, the Lafleur farmhouse was not on any of them. But based on the landmarks he remembered, and the time he'd spent journeying with his Resistance guides, the three had been able to estimate the general area where René's home had to be. Were they right? It was impossible to guess. But the attack on Sainte-Régine—and many lives—depended on the answer.

Jacob made his way along the lane, squinting through the gloom, searching for anything that seemed man-made. A barn loomed up ahead. Excitedly, he quickened his pace. There was the house. Through the window, he could make out the dim glow of a dying fireplace. This had to be it!

He hesitated. Something was off. Of course, he had spent much more time *underneath* René's home than standing outside looking at it. But this just wasn't the place. The pitch of the roof was too steep, the structure too small.

Disappointment flooded over him, tinged with a little panic. Of all the contingencies they'd planned for, he and the captain had never talked about what would happen if he simply couldn't find René and his Resistance comrades.

On he slogged, his spirits plunging. A second farmhouse

appeared half a kilometer farther on, but it seemed wrong too. Come to think of it, maybe the first place was right after all, and he'd been too mixed up to recognize it. Should he go back? Or venture on to a third house?

He caught a whiff of something in the air—a cooking smell. Chicken stew, only burnt. A smile of pure wonder spread across his face. It had to be Madame Lafleur—she burned everything! She had led him home with her questionable kitchen skills.

He paused at the edge of the trees, poised like a pointer for a full five minutes. No one must see an American soldier entering this home. Finally, keeping low to the shadows, he approached the house and stepped up onto the porch. A board creaked underfoot.

In a split second, the door flew open and someone came up behind him and twisted his arm in a hammerlock, a knife at his throat.

And then Madame appeared in the doorway. "René—*non! C'est* Jacob!"

Jacob was dragged into the house and hustled down to the root cellar.

René was angry. "You take a great risk coming back here, monsieur!"

"My captain sent me," Jacob explained. "We can help each other."

Jacob told the Resistance leader about the upcoming American attack, and the problem with the big artillery piece that was menacing the single approach to Sainte-Régine.

"We hear this gun from time to time," René confirmed. "But we did not know it was right in the town. It must be well hidden."

"Can you find it?" Jacob asked pointedly.

"Sainte-Régine is our town" was René's reply. "So long have we waited for the Americans to come and rid us of the Boches. I will destroy this gun if I have to crush the barrel with my own teeth."

"It'll be easier if you use this." Jacob shrugged out of his backpack and opened it. It was filled with small gray bricks of high explosive.

René's eyes gleamed in appreciation. "For us in the Resistance, this is like Christmas morning."

By the light of a single candle in the secret root cellar where Jacob had been nursed back to health, the American private and the Resistance leader went over the plans for the attack, which was scheduled for the day after tomorrow. Jacob provided grim details of the wounded men on the hospital truck—that would be Bravo Company if the Resistance couldn't locate and disable the big gun. Without that critical step, the liberation of Sainte-Régine was destined to fail.

Long into the night, they discussed the possibilities. Then they synchronized watches and embraced warmly, promising to meet again when Sainte-Régine was free at last.

"You're a good luck charm, little Jacob," René said, beaming. "It was worth my effort to pick you up out of that ditch." He pulled the ring with the double-barred cross from his finger and pressed it into Jacob's palm. "You are one of us now."

It was a gesture Jacob would remember for a lifetime. "I'll always treasure this," he promised emotionally, slipping it into his pocket.

Madame kissed him roundly on both cheeks, and wept a few motherly tears. Then he was on his way.

By this time, it was close to dawn, and he had to hurry to make it to the rendezvous point before sunrise. It was the kind of dark that only happens just before first light, so the most speed he could risk was a light jog. In his mind, he was already in the jeep that would carry him back to camp and Captain Marone.

The plan was a go! The fact that he, Jacob Firestone, had made it happen filled him with an excitement that brought him all the way back to the recruiting center in New Haven. *This* was why he had enlisted in the first place—to make a difference. Sure, he understood that he'd done his share countless times in this war. But as one soldier of hundreds of thousands. This was something else—an operation that couldn't have happened without him. A whole town would be liberated thanks to his actions.

Lost in the exhilaration of his thoughts, Jacob never noticed the pale face until it was just a few feet in front of him. A German soldier, helmetless, blond, and every bit as shocked as Jacob himself. Jacob could smell alcohol on the man's breath, and noticed an open bottle of wine in his hand.

The two stood there, eyes locked. The German had a rifle slung over his shoulder, but he made no move. Nor did Jacob reach for the pistol in his holster. They stared at each other for a long moment. The German didn't seem to know what to do. He was probably drunk, and maybe in a place he wasn't supposed to be. Jacob was definitely where *he* wasn't supposed to be. Captain Marone's words came back to him once more: *If you get caught, there's nothing we can do for you.*

Worse still, if he got caught, the liberation of Sainte-Régine might never happen.

Hand trembling, Jacob pointed to himself and then pointed across the road into the orchard. He waited, breathless, for his enemy's response.

The German's eyes widened a little. It was impossible to be certain, but he seemed to be thinking it over. He wanted to be out of this standoff just as much as Jacob did. When it finally came, his nod of agreement was so slight that Jacob was unsure whether or not he'd actually seen it. But the alternative— standing here until daylight—was not an option. The German had that advantage: They were on *his* side of the line.

Jacob then did something that the army had been warning him not to do ever since Fort Benning: He turned his back on an armed enemy.

With every step through the soft earth of the orchard, Jacob braced himself for the crack of the rifle and the impact of the bullet that would end his life.

Neither came.

He did not risk a look back. When he was far enough into the trees and out of range, Jacob ran like he'd never run before.

CHAPTER TWENTY-SIX

SAINTE-RÉGINE, FRANCE— SEPTEMBER 12, 1944

Less than thirty-six hours later, the Battle of Sainte-Régine had begun. Jacob pressed his back against a tree trunk, watching the two medics carrying off the injured Beau.

"You take good care of him!" he shouted. He couldn't even hear himself over the roar of the American artillery passing overhead, and the answering pound of the big gun in the village.

On the narrow road leading into town, soldiers of the armored unit struggled to move aside the two burning Sherman tanks. Treads smashed, the disabled bulldozer that had been sent to clear a path was itself in need of clearing. Behind the snarl, all the American tanks and vehicles were trapped, sitting ducks waiting for the Sainte-Régine gun to cut them to pieces.

Where was René? Where was the Resistance? Why couldn't that weapon be silenced before it wiped out the entire invasion force? Like the hedgerows of Normandy, the mature apple trees in this orchard provided the greatest natural defense in the history of warfare. So much so that a single gun raining shells down on the road could stop an entire army. Jacob thought back to the wounded men on the hospital truck they had passed on the way to Sainte-Régine. Would that be Bravo Company's fate?

Lieutenant McCoy was still yelling, urging the infantrymen to ignore the disaster on the road and advance through the trees. But there was little stomach to take on the enemy without the armor support the entire attack was based upon.

"Where are your Resistance friends?" McCoy shouted at Jacob. "Why's that big gun still shooting at us?"

Dismayed by Beau's injury and the destruction on the road, Jacob could only stare back at his lieutenant.

McCoy rolled his eyes. "What do you expect when you pin your whole plan on a high school kid?" He ran ahead, still bellowing instructions.

Jacob was stunned. Was the lieutenant saying that all this was his fault? Obviously, Jacob couldn't be held responsible for the German defenses or the topography of Sainte-Régine. But the idea to rely on René and his Resistance fighters—that had been 100 percent Jacob.

What was the delay? René and his people were supposed to have acted two hours ago. Could they not find the gun? Or was it so well guarded that they couldn't get to it? Had they been captured or killed?

The awful thoughts buzzed through Jacob's head, drowning out even the overhead screaming of the shells. He hefted his rifle and took off through the orchard, keeping low to the ground. By the time he passed his lieutenant, he was sprinting.

"There you go, Firestone!" he called at first. Then, a moment later, "Hey, not so fast!"

Jacob did not slow down. Something had gone wrong, and it was up to him to get to the bottom of it.

The three French Resistance fighters wore dark trench coats and stocking caps as they made their way through the streets. They had little fear of being arrested by the Boches—not now that the battle was under way. Most of the garrison had advanced into the orchard to engage the Allied attackers. The biggest danger was the incoming fire from the American artillery. Every now and then, a shell would slam into the town, and a moment later, an entire building would collapse in on itself. Those few Germans who remained in the village were busy supervising the local fire brigade fighting the blazes caused by the bombardment.

The three had heard of towns around France that had suffered this kind of destruction. Was their beloved Sainte-Régine next? What on earth was the point of liberating a town that was nothing but rubble?

If only they could find the gun they'd been sent to destroy. That would allow the Americans in, which would have the added bonus of putting a stop to the artillery barrage. The Resistance men looked around in anguish. This mission had been doomed from the start. René, their leader, had not turned up at the rendezvous point. They had waited for him until the battle had begun, but could wait no longer.

Their hearts were heavy. Their leader's absence did not bode well. If René was not here to be part of this operation, then something terrible must have happened.

But there was still the mission, and they would strive to complete it, with him or without him. Sainte-Régine was not a large town. How could such a powerful artillery piece escape their notice? They could hear it, even feel its concussion as it fired down on the Americans. The three knew a grudging respect for the hated Boches for having hidden this weapon so completely that even the townspeople could not locate it.

And then, the youngest of the men pointed to a puff of smoke rising from a broken skylight in the abandoned stables at the edge of the village.

"Look!"

Hugging walls and staying in the shadows, they snaked their way through the town, approaching the old livery stable from the rear. As they crept toward the door, an earth-shattering blast rattled every board in the ancient structure. Looking up, they were actually able to see the shell bursting through the broken skylight and sailing out over the orchards toward the American positions.

The three exchanged knowing glances. The big gun was hidden inside the stable.

No words were exchanged. They communicated by a series of hand signals. Pistols were drawn. Expressions hardened with the knowledge that it would be necessary to kill the gun crew. Then they would blow up the weapon with the RDX putty explosive the young American had provided.

The three did not relish the violence that lay ahead, nor were they afraid of it. The men and women of the French Resistance did what needed to be done, without question or judgment.

But when they eased open the sliding door to peer inside, an astounding sight met their eyes. There was no gun crew, no giant artillery piece. Instead, they found themselves looking at the armored hulk of a German Tiger tank, its cannon pointed out the open skylight.

The mysterious gun was not a gun at all—at least not *just* a gun. It was a tank, the largest battlefield weapon in the German arsenal. No wonder its devastating effect had been mistaken for an artillery piece. Its 88-millimeter cannon was capable of hitting targets three kilometers away with a frightening degree of accuracy. The entire road leading into Sainte-Régine lay under the threat of this instrument of destruction.

Their plan had to change, but in many ways it would become easier. There would be no shoot-out with a gun crew. Instead, if they acted quietly and stealthily, they might be able to destroy the tank with the soldiers inside never becoming aware of their presence.

Careful to avoid the viewing port at the front of the tank, the Resistance men slipped into the stable. They distributed the bricks of explosive among the three of them and set to work molding the RDX putty to the body of the tank. They had to resist the temptation to pack the explosive around the base of the gun itself. That would put them too close to the viewing port and alert the crew to their presence. No, they had to hope that the American had provided enough RDX to put the entire tank out of commission.

At last, they attached the detonator wires and prepared to step away.

And then, as had happened countless times in the history of warfare, random chance took over. A member of the German tank crew decided to come out to smoke a cigarette. The hatch was flung open and a blond head emerged.

It was so unexpected that the three froze for an instant. The Boche was shocked as well, but his recovery was quicker. A black Luger appeared in his hand, he spat twice, and one of the three Frenchmen was dead. The other two fired back, killing the German, who tumbled down the side of the tank to the stable floor.

But the damage was done. Agitated shouts erupted from inside the Tiger.

The youngest Frenchman fumbled with the detonator, but hesitated for a fatal second. If he set off the explosive here, at close range, they would all die in a fireball.

The pause proved his undoing. A second Boche appeared at the hatchway, and this one had a machine gun. The young Frenchman was sprayed with bullets. The plunger flew out of his hand and skittered across the weathered planks.

The last of the Resistance fighters dove for it, but the German had the same idea, dropping the gun and leaping down onto the Frenchman. They wrestled for the detonator, a life-and-death struggle, each shouting in a language the other did not understand. The Resistance man was bigger and stronger, but the Boche was younger, and at the peak of his training. They rolled around on the floor, both men jockeying for advantage.

A roar followed by the screech of gears filled the stable. It signified that the tank commander had decided to flee whatever danger threatened his Tiger. The armored hulk trembled for a moment before the treads began to move forward.

On the floor, both men took in the horrifying sight of tons of machinery bearing down on them. Too late, they let go of each other.

They were not able to get out of the way in time.

CHAPTER TWENTY-SEVEN

SAINTE-RÉGINE, FRANCE— SEPTEMBER 12, 1944

Jacob's lungs were on fire as he pounded through the orchard, his rifle held out in front of him, jerking wildly with each crazed step. He could see the outskirts of the town through the trees ahead of him, which meant that somehow, he had managed to crash through the German lines without encountering a single defender. Good luck—or maybe not. He could hear rifle and machine-gun fire behind him as Bravo Company battled the enemy he'd somehow evaded. At this point, the shot that brought him down would very likely come from one of his own people, or from the artillery barrage that was still dropping shells on the town.

Running past enemy lines didn't seem like such a great idea anymore. But now that he was here, he had to find out what had happened to René and his mission. German shells were still falling on the road into town. Until that stopped, the American armor would never be able to advance into Sainte-Régine.

As he emerged from the cover of the trees, his training kicked back in and he flattened himself to the ground, surveying the surrounding buildings, searching for snipers. Nobody shot at him. Carefully he crawled to a wooden fence and got to his feet again, peering through a gap in the boards.

Spying a German uniform, he sighted along his rifle and prepared to fire. Then he realized that the enemy soldier was supervising a bucket brigade of citizens battling a house fire. He didn't dare shoot without risking hitting one of them.

Where was the big gun? That was the real question. How could such a devastating weapon be so completely hidden in a French village half the size of Jacob's hometown in Connecticut?

Calm down, High School, Beau would have said if he'd been there. *Don't go running off half-cocked. Think this out!*

Struggling to calm his hammering heart, he surveyed what he could see of Sainte-Régine. The downtown consisted of streets of old cottages and, at the center, row houses around a cathedral and an open square. That was it. You'd have trouble hiding a Chevy roadster in this place, much less a devastating artillery cannon. And before you knew it, you were out of this one-horse town—his eyes settled on an ancient wooden structure that looked like an oversized barn.

As he stared at it, trying to figure out what it was, or what it might be hiding, the entire front wall disintegrated into toothpicks. There was the roar of a very large engine, and out of the cloud of dust rolled a gigantic German tank.

A Tiger! Jacob thought to himself in horror. *Captain Marone never said anything about a Tiger tank in Sainte-Régine!*

His eyes fixed on the huge machine's 88-millimeter cannon and light dawned. No wonder nobody had been able to find the mystery artillery piece menacing the road. It wasn't artillery at all.

He frowned. Even at a distance, he could see that there was some kind of interruption to the dark camouflage pattern of the tank's hulk. He squinted. It looked as if the armored side had been slathered with mud—but how would that happen to a vehicle hidden inside a building?

He ran to the cover of a small shed and peered around the corner for a closer view. There was something familiar about the slate-gray color of the "mud." Jacob had seen it before—formed into bricks and encased in protective wrap in his backpack. That wasn't mud; it was RDX putty—the high explosive he had provided to René!

Jacob's mind raced. So René's Resistance cell had gone on the mission after all. They'd found the Tiger and realized that it was the gun they'd been looking for. They'd even molded the explosive to the body of the tank to blow it up. But why hadn't they followed through?

Something had gone wrong. They must have been caught deploying the RDX, and wound up captured or killed before they could set it off. He sat back on his heels and tried to work out what this meant. It didn't take Albert Einstein. Any way he twisted it around in his mind, the answer always came out the same: Mrs. Firestone's little boy was now in charge of taking out that Tiger tank.

It was impossible. No lone soldier could destroy a tank, much less the most powerful one on earth. But this particular tank was already covered in high explosive. All Jacob had to do was find a way to set it off.

The RDX putty was detonated by a small plunger he'd given to René, but that could have been anywhere at this point. No matter how hard he racked his brain, he couldn't recall any plan B from his training on how to ignite high explosives. He did remember something about a detonator providing a spark. Surely a bullet slamming into the armor of the tank would do the same thing.

With the stock of his rifle pressed against his shoulder, he scrambled out from the cover of the shed and ran across the hard-packed dirt terrain. About thirty meters from the Tiger, he dropped to one knee and opened fire. The first bullet ripped into the gray putty and ricocheted off the armor with a clang. He shot three more, all direct hits. They only served to knock chunks of explosive off the side of the tank.

And then, the big turret began to swing around in his direction. It moved so slowly that he was almost mesmerized watching it turn toward him. By the time he sprang into action, he was practically staring straight down the barrel.

Jacob was never sure exactly how he got out of the way—just that when the big gun fired, he wasn't standing there anymore. Nothing was there except a giant, smoking crater in the dirt, and Jacob was flat on his face about ten meters away, his ears throbbing with pain at the noise of the blast.

Something was digging into his hip—more pain. He knew he had to get away. The turret was already moving in his new direction. He reached down to the sore spot and found what was digging into his flesh. It was a hand grenade.

Something clicked in his fevered mind. Rifle bullets weren't producing the spark he needed, but an exploding grenade . . .

He leaped to his feet and pulled the pin with his teeth. Then came the hard part—counting out the seconds as the 88-millimeter cannon pivoted to reacquire him. At Fort Benning, the sergeants had told them to count to five before throwing. But this grenade had to go off in the air as close as possible to the RDX.

Four . . . five . . .

Throw it, High School! Beau was not there, but Jacob heard his voice as clear as if his friend had been standing at his shoulder.

Six . . . seven . . .

The barrel of the giant gun found him again and locked on.

Eight . . .

Jacob chucked the grenade, while at the same time hurling himself backward and to the side.

The grenade detonated just as it was coming down onto the side of the Tiger. Jacob heard it go off. Then there was an explosion that was much, much larger.

He felt a massive wave of heat pass over him and he remembered very little after that. The next thing he knew, the tank was completely engulfed in flames. There was no sign of life inside it.

He had no idea how long he'd been unconscious. In a daze, he picked himself up off the ground and looked around. Members of Bravo Company were coming out of the woods, leading groups of German prisoners. In the distance, he could see the road. The armored column was on the move, approaching town.

"I did it," he blurted aloud.

It wasn't a boast or even a simple statement of pride. He

said it in sheer amazement. Almost nothing had gone according to plan, but the basic strategy had worked. With the big gun silenced, the Americans had a clear path into Sainte-Régine. René's beloved village was free.

René! Jacob picked up his rifle, slung it over his shoulder, and, half jogging, half limping, shambled to what was left of the barnlike structure that had been the Tiger's hiding place. Upon closer inspection, he could see that it had once been a stable. Now, of course, it was fit only for the wrecking ball. An entire wall was missing and parts of it were burning—a sure sign of just how large the tank's explosion must have been. Jacob was lucky he hadn't blown himself up too—along with half the town.

A grisly discovery awaited him inside. There were five bodies on the floor of the stable—two German soldiers and three men in dark clothing who must have been Resistance fighters. Two of them—one from each side—appeared to have been crushed by the tank. Jacob swallowed hard. No matter how much he saw of war, he couldn't seem to get used to it. Maybe that was a good thing.

The detonator plunger lay close by. That would have come in handy. No sign of René. Did that mean the Resistance leader had escaped the fate of his three comrades? Jacob had to find out.

Rejoining his unit never even occurred to him. He ran across the small town, ignoring the shouts from the stray members of the German garrison who were looking for an American to surrender to. As he ran past the vanguard of the armored column, crew members called out to him in concern.

"Hey, buddy, you need a ride?"

"We've got medics in the truck back there!"

For the first time, Jacob took stock of the state he was in. His uniform was filthy and tattered, smoldering in places, but too muddy to burn. His pants were torn at one hip, and he could feel warm blood trickling down his thigh. Something from the explosion had struck him—something small, since he wasn't badly wounded. It didn't hurt—or maybe the problem was that his entire body hurt, this one area no more than any other. But even if there was a German V-2 rocket lodged in there, it wasn't going to keep Jacob from getting to the farmhouse. He wouldn't let it. Reaching René was his one thought, his one purpose.

A few minutes later, he actually jogged past Captain Marone in a jeep, but his commanding officer failed to recognize him.

By the time he made it to the dirt lane that led through the orchards to the local farms, Jacob could already see the dense black plume coming from somewhere ahead. He had been in a daze ever since the explosion of the Tiger had knocked him out, but now reality returned in the form of a churning dread in the pit of his stomach. The smoke could have been caused by anything—a brush fire or burning trash. But he just knew.

The farmhouse was gone, burned to the ground. All that remained was a brick chimney where Madame's kitchen had once stood. Jacob broke into a run and limped up to the still-burning ruin. René sat cross-legged on the ground, facing the wreckage but not quite seeing it, his disbelieving eyes focused on some point a hundred miles away.

"What happened?" Jacob managed, his voice raw.

René looked at him—looked right through him, really.

"The Boches. This is what they do to us—to the Resistance."

"But the children! Madame!"

The Frenchman indicated the smoldering rubble. "All gone. It was a risk we accepted willingly. Today I am not so willing. Four years our secret stayed safe. I should have known it would not last forever."

Standing there, awash in this man's grief, Jacob was assaulted by a murky vision from two nights before. A pale face in a German uniform coming upon him as he made his way back to Bravo Company from the final meeting with René. Jacob had been so grateful to have escaped the soldier, to have avoided a deadly shoot-out. Even as he'd run off into the orchard, he'd fully expected a bullet between his shoulder blades. He'd been so relieved that he'd immediately put the encounter out of his mind. Never had it occurred to him that the German might have been able to identify the farmhouse he'd been coming from. It seemed so obvious now that an enemy soldier's visit would finger the house as Resistance.

It was like a lightning strike. He should have known. Somewhere in his brain, he *must* have known! Why had he ignored the obvious danger? He'd been happy just to survive. And in his joy, he had doomed Madame and the children and destroyed René.

Never taking his eyes off the wreckage of his home, René murmured, almost as an afterthought, "Sainte-Régine is free?"

"Free," Jacob confirmed. "The German garrison surrendered." But even as he was delivering this good news, tears were streaming down his cheeks. "René—it was—it was *me*."

Weeping openly, he told the story of his chance meeting with the drunken German soldier. "He let me go. But he must have seen the house I'd come from."

Slowly, the Resistance leader got to his feet and turned to face Jacob.

"I'm sorry!" Jacob sobbed. "I'm so, *so* sorry!"

When René spoke, his tone was oddly formal, like a government official making a proclamation. "I thank you for helping to save my village. But I must not lay eyes on you again. Do you understand?"

Wordlessly, Jacob nodded. His eyes still blurred with tears, he turned and stumbled away. Not even when they'd lost Freddie and Leland and so many others had he felt such deep despair. That had been the fortunes of war, tragic yet unavoidable. Even expected.

But this had been his fault—his carelessness, his stupidity. René and his family had saved his life, nursed him back to health. And he had repaid them by bringing disaster down on their heads. And the worst part: There was nothing he could do to make it right.

As he stalked through the orchard, he cursed the day he'd enlisted in the army. He'd wanted to make a difference. Well, he'd certainly managed that. Madame would burn no more meals. The children would not grow up. And René would never be the same.

Wrapped up in the turmoil of his thoughts, he almost missed the sound of running feet. Suddenly alert, he reached for his rifle, but before he could pull it from his shoulder, a

German uniform burst out of the underbrush. Acting on pure instinct, Jacob stuck out a leg. The enemy soldier tripped over it and tumbled to the ground. By the time he got to his knees, Jacob was standing over him, rifle pointed.

The rage Jacob experienced was something new. He'd known fear and adrenaline in battle, but this was sheer, unadulterated hatred. This was not the soldier who had killed René's family, but he was one of *them*, and he would do. Just a moment before, Jacob had been lost in despair. Yet as his misery morphed into anger, he felt *better*, because now he had purpose—and the purpose was vengeance. This enemy was going to pay for Madame and the children—and for Freddie and Leland and all the others too.

He stared down the rifle barrel and saw—*himself.* Not Jacob Firestone, but pale blue eyes that reminded him very much of the teenage boy he faced in the mirror every day. In another life, they could have been twelfth graders together, swapping chemistry notes and talking about girls. He felt his finger loosening on the trigger.

No! he exhorted himself. *You walked away from an enemy in this orchard once before and look what happened! You can't let this one go!*

But when Jacob sighted down at the boy, he beheld no menace, only terror. There had been so much death and suffering already. What could possibly be gained by killing this poor scared kid in the aftermath of a battle that was already over?

Jacob lowered his rifle. "Get out of here, High School. Beat it."

And when the stunned boy scrambled up, gawked at him in disbelief, and ran off, Jacob felt reborn.

CHAPTER TWENTY-EIGHT

SAINTE-RÉGINE, FRANCE—MAY 5

If the *portier* hadn't opened the heavy brass doors of Au Toit Rouge, Trevor might have blasted right through them. That was how fast he was moving in an effort to put as much distance as possible between himself and his father and great-grandfather.

Once clear of the building, he kept on sprinting, heedless of direction—a left turn at the café on the corner, a right turn at the bookstore, straight on past the old stone cathedral. The only destination that mattered was away.

Where could you go when everything you'd ever believed in was turned upside down? Certainly nowhere in Sainte-Régine, the place where it had all happened.

A baby stroller was thrust in front of Trevor. He nearly dislocated every joint in his body in an effort to stop before he flattened it. A young mother scolded him in angry French, and he apologized in halting English, sidestepping and moving off quickly.

Jacob Firestone—not a hero! Worse, practically a *villain*! A hero wannabe whose carelessness wiped out an entire family! Never in a million years could Trevor have imagined anything like this to be true. And yet he had heard it from G.G.'s own mouth.

"But, Grandpa," Dad had pleaded with the old man back at the hotel, "that wasn't your fault. You were just a kid! You couldn't have been expected to know what was going to happen."

G.G. was adamant. "I could have been expected to follow my training, and to remember the things I'd been seeing ever since I'd set foot in Europe. I could have been expected to have half the brains God gave geese. But instead I was an idiot. A lot of innocent people paid the price for it, and I wasn't one of them. Tomorrow, I'm going to tell them to save their medal for someone who deserves it."

Trevor shook his head to clear it, but it did nothing to stop the whirling of his mind. Had they honestly traveled to Fort Benning, London, and all across France for G.G. to get a medal he wasn't even going to accept? Surely this hadn't been his great-grandfather's plan all along! It couldn't have been. G.G. had been having a fantastic time on the trip—at least at first. But the closer they'd gotten to Sainte-Régine, the more the weight of all this had started to press down on the old man. On the other hand, Dad said that the threatening messages from La Vérité had started even before they'd left Connecticut. Dad hadn't understood their full meaning, but G.G. should have.

What a mess! The trip of a lifetime had turned into a disaster. Here they were, thousands of miles from home for G.G. to get an honor he didn't deserve and no longer wanted. Hardest to accept was that the awful girl and boy who'd been dogging their movements had been right all along! Jacob Firestone was no hero—and nobody agreed with that more than Jacob Firestone himself.

The thought of home made Trevor yearn to see Mom—and even his kid sisters, Kira and Kelsey. But when he pictured his bedroom, it struck another discordant note. The walls were covered with posters and pictures of World War II, and for some reason, they just didn't seem *right* anymore. Even though he'd been born decades after it had ended, the war had always been the center of Trevor's life. He was the great-grandson of a war hero, and even though he and G.G. were far apart in age, they'd always been best friends. He played video games based on the war, built models from it, read books and watched movies about it. He thought about it, dreamed about it, imagined what it must have been like to be there. In school, he never handed in a social studies project on any other subject. World War II was the largest single event in history, and a lot of people considered it humankind's greatest achievement—that so many whole countries could team up to fight against evil. Even now, Trevor felt that way with all his heart.

But he had always pictured the war as a gigantic chess match, played by generals, using pieces that represented armies. Everything went like clockwork. You executed your strategy, conquered territory, defeated your enemies.

He still believed World War II was *right*. Yet now it seemed more like a wheel of fortune, where the difference between life and death was pure luck. Whole cities could be sacrificed because they happened to be in the wrong place at the wrong time. The bombs falling on you could be coming from your own planes as easily as those of your enemy. You could make it across the deadliest expanse of Omaha Beach, only to put your foot down on a mine as soon as you'd reached semi-safety. And perhaps worst of all was what happened to G.G., where a tiny lapse of judgment resulted in the deaths of innocents—your mistake, your fault, end of story.

Chaos was the word G.G. had once used to describe war. It looked cool on a movie screen or in a video game. But when real lives were being lost, snuffed out by sheer random chance, there was no glory.

There had been no glory three-quarters of a century ago in Sainte-Régine for Private Jacob Firestone. And Trevor could see that his great-grandfather would be haunted by it until the end of his life.

He was pretty lost by then, but he knew he'd be able to find Au Toit Rouge. Sainte-Régine was so small, and the cathedral towered over everything, like a beacon that would guide him to the hotel. Upset as he was, he would have to go back eventually. It was a long way to Connecticut, and Dad had the tickets and passports.

Trevor took one more corner and practically ran into her. The blond girl was walking briskly in the opposite direction. They both froze for a moment, staring at each other.

"Don't run away," Trevor told her.

"I did not throw that stone!" She stuck her chin out defiantly, expecting an accusation.

"I believe you. But I also believe you know who did. Your friend with the motorcycle?"

"My cousin, Philippe," she admitted. "I am Juliette. Lafleur—perhaps you have heard this name?"

"I've heard it," Trevor replied gravely. "From G.G.—from my great-grandfather. A man he once knew—René Lafleur."

"*My* great-grandfather," she confirmed. "The only survivor."

"G.G. also told me about La Vérité. That's you, right? And your cousin, the hall-of-fame pitcher?"

"Excuse me?"

"It takes a pretty big arm to heave a cobblestone that size through a window three stories up. What do you want from us?"

"Is this not obvious?" she asked emotionally. "We do not want your G.G. to be honored in our town. Why do you think we formed La Vérité and posted warnings? Why do you think we traveled to Normandy and followed you across France?"

Trevor was amazed. "But how did you find us? France is a big place."

Juliette offered a rueful smile. "How could we not? You Americans describe every move you make on your Instagram. We knew when your boat would arrive in Cherbourg, and each place you would visit thereafter. You have a fine eye for detail, but you make a poor secret agent."

"All to get revenge on a ninety-three-year-old man," Jacob concluded resentfully.

"No, not revenge. We wanted to persuade him to stay in America. And when he arrived in Cherbourg, we wanted him to change his mind and go home. After what he did to our family, he does not deserve to be honored." She let out a heavy sigh. "But now that you are here, we merely wish the ceremony to be over, and you to be gone."

Trevor nodded. "I get that. You'd probably be surprised to hear that G.G. doesn't think he deserves to be honored either."

She flushed with anger. "Then why are you here? Did we not make it clear enough that the 'hero' of Sainte-Régine was not wanted? When we vandalized your car and your hotel rooms, did you think we were the welcoming committee?"

Trevor shrugged unhappily. "I can't figure out why he wanted to come. I don't know what to think anymore. Maybe he felt that by coming here, he could somehow make amends for what happened. I'll tell you one thing, though—that quiet, weak, unhappy old man is *not* the great-grandfather I grew up with. G.G. is strong, and lively, and funny, and loud. There isn't anything he doesn't have an opinion about. He's my favorite person in the entire world—or at least he used to be. But the closer we got to here, the more his guilt came crashing down on him. And if it's Sainte-Régine that's turning him into a shadow of himself, then I want him out of here twice as much as you do."

He waited for an angry retort. It didn't come. Instead, Juliette said, "So we have something in common, you and I. We want this to be over. A Lafleur and a Firestone in agreement. Who would believe it?"

"Maybe *we* want the same thing," Trevor pointed out, "but can you say that for everybody else? That ceremony tomorrow is right out in the open. I have to know that G.G. will be safe. How many members of La Vérité are there?"

Juliette's reply was bitter. "You continue to miss the point. We are not many, we Lafleurs, thanks to your G.G. The many aunts, uncles, and cousins we would have today—never born. So you need not fear the armies of La Vérité. There are but two of us. Me and—" She stopped short.

"Cousin Philippe," Trevor finished.

Her expression was suddenly distressed, and she spoke in an anxious voice. "Philippe is not a bad person, but he will not put the past behind him as I have decided to do. I begged him not to throw that stone. He would not listen."

"Do you think he'll try to bust up the ceremony tomorrow?" Trevor asked anxiously.

"I fear so. He is very angry."

"We have to call the police!" Trevor urged.

"No!" Her tone was strident. "He is what you Americans call a hothead. But I will not have Philippe arrested over what he *might* do."

"That's easy for you to say," Trevor shot back. "I know you love your cousin, but think how much damage one of those cobblestones could do to somebody's *head*—especially an old man. That wouldn't be good for Philippe either. He'd get sent to Devil's Island."

Juliette laughed in his face. "You see too many movies. Nobody gets sent to Devil's Island anymore. And in case you are wondering, we no longer have the guillotine."

"Okay, you don't like G.G.," Trevor concluded. "And

maybe he did an awful thing. But remember this—he was only here because he came from thousands of miles away to fight for France. Nobody made him. He *volunteered*. So he's a hero for *that*, anyway—him and Beau and Leland and Freddie . . ."

She looked shocked, and he realized that two tears had spilled over and were trickling down his cheeks. He had so much more to say—about how the young soldiers had risked their lives every day, and how Freddie and Leland had made the ultimate sacrifice. But he didn't want to blubber all over her. So he finished with, "You know how old G.G. was when he fought here? Seventeen."

"Philippe is seventeen," she whispered.

They stood there, facing each other, for what seemed like a long time. Trevor was breathing hard from the effort to keep his emotions in check; Juliette was lost in thought.

Finally she spoke up. "I'm sorry, Trevor. I cannot inform the police."

"But who's going to protect G.G. if something bad happens?"

"*We* will. You and I."

CHAPTER TWENTY-NINE

SAINTE-RÉGINE, FRANCE—MAY 6

Dad pulled the end of the tie through the Windsor knot and tightened it at Trevor's collar. "There. You look almost human."

Trevor winced. "I feel like I'm strangling."

Dad fiddled with his own shirt. "Me too," he admitted. "That's one of the perks to being a teacher—you don't have to wear a suit." He turned serious. "You're okay with this, right, Trev? I know what G.G. told us yesterday must have been pretty upsetting to you."

It was the morning of the ceremony honoring Private First Class Jacob Firestone, the hero of Sainte-Régine, and the three were up early in the suite, getting ready. A local cleaner had volunteered to press their dress clothes, which were crushed and wrinkled after the better part of two weeks packed away in suitcases. Now their shirts were so heavily starched that they could barely move. G.G. was still in the bathroom, shaving, but they knew they were going to hear about it from him. He wasn't a big fan of "monkey suits."

"I'll be okay," Trevor assured his father. "I walked it off yesterday."

He had already decided not to say a word to Dad and G.G. about his meeting and conversation with Juliette Lafleur. The last thing they needed to know was that Juliette's psycho cousin was out there somewhere, planning to attack the ceremony and probably G.G. himself. The old soldier was freaked out enough already, just by remembering the past.

This trip should have been a win-win for G.G.—to reexperience the most exciting and meaningful part of his life, capped off by having glory heaped upon him by a whole town. Who would have believed that a seventeen-year-old soldier, who should have been in high school, could make one tiny error in judgment that would come back to haunt him more than seventy-five years later?

Dad sighed. "At least it'll be over soon. If Grandpa can keep it together long enough to take his medal and say thanks— or no thanks—then we can get out of here. I'm positive that once he's away from this place with so many loaded memories, he'll be his old self again."

Yeah, Trevor thought to himself. *But will I ever be my old self again?*

So much of his identity came from his fascination with World War II and from his connection to it, through G.G. Now that was gone—or at least *different*. And he felt empty, like a part of him had gone missing.

Trevor regarded his father expectantly. It had to be coming—Dad's I-told-you-so lecture about his son's obsession with war and G.G.'s war stories. But for some reason, Dad wasn't in a gloating mood. Or maybe Daniel Firestone was even more upset by G.G.'s revelations than Trevor was. After all, Dad was the one who had grown up in the old man's house.

The last couple of days couldn't have been easy on him either.

A snort of laughter from the doorway interrupted that train of thought.

"Ha—are you two getting married in those suits?"

G.G. wore jeans and a warm-up jacket.

"Grandpa!" Dad exclaimed. "Where's your suit?"

"In the closet where it belongs," the old man growled. "I'm not getting dressed up like an undertaker and pretending to be the hero I'm not."

"I understand you have mixed emotions," Dad said gently. "But these people are coming out to honor you, and you owe it to them to let yourself be honored."

G.G.'s voice was bitter. "Well, so long as *they're* happy . . ."

Dad was adamant. "Their town was occupied by the Nazis, and then it wasn't anymore, thanks to the efforts and sacrifice of an American unit. You're the last surviving member of that unit. Nothing can change that."

Trevor blinked. Dad believed that? And was that a small note of pride in his voice?

G.G. looked at his great-grandson. "Does he push you around like that?" But he took his suit into the bedroom to change.

When the old man was dressed, Dad helped pin on the various medals and combat ribbons G.G. had been awarded during the war. Over the years, Trevor had seen them all in their cases, but this was his first view of his great-grandfather decked out in full military regalia. It was an impressive sight— until he took in G.G.'s sunken eyes, grayish pallor, and the slumped shoulders that had replaced the old soldier's normally ramrod-straight posture.

Dad was determined to stay positive. "You look wonderful, Grandpa."

"Let's get this over with," G.G. said through clenched teeth.

The whole thing was what the old man would have called "a dog and pony show." As soon as they stepped off the hotel elevator into the lobby, the waiting employees burst into applause. Parked at the curb was a horse-drawn carriage, strewn with flowers.

"That's one way to spruce up your town for a party," G.G. whispered to Trevor as they clip-clopped toward the central square. "Spread around some horse manure."

Trevor snickered a little. It was a trace of the old G.G., who had been all too absent lately. Mostly, Trevor was too tense to laugh. He peered left and right, trying to catch a glimpse of Juliette amid the throngs of people who had come for the ceremony. She was out there somewhere, keeping her eyes peeled for Philippe.

Sainte-Régine's central square was resplendent in red, white, and blue—although technically, half of it counted as blue, white, and red, the French *tricolore*. American and French flags were everywhere, and the raised platform where the ceremony would take place was decorated with bunting.

The mayor himself was there to greet Jacob Firestone. Trevor's hand was pumped again and again as he was introduced to a lineup of dignitaries, including a handful of senior citizens who had been in Sainte-Régine in 1944 on liberation day. They all had complicated names that Trevor wouldn't have been able to pronounce even if he could have remembered them. He and his father exchanged a nervous glance. The old soldier was meeting people and exchanging small talk in English. He was a shadow of his regular self, but of course, the town officials had no way of knowing that. So far so good.

As they were escorted onto the platform, Trevor had his first chance to survey the crowd. Oh man, there were a lot of people here! Hundreds—maybe even more than a thousand. It was proof that G.G.'s visit after all these years was a very big deal to the locals. But how was Trevor ever going to spot Juliette in this mob? And more to the point, how were the two of them going to find Philippe before he did something terrible?

His phone vibrated in his blazer pocket and he grabbed it eagerly. He and Juliette had exchanged numbers yesterday.

Her text message was on the screen: *Nice suit.*

He thumbed: *Where ru?* On second thought, he changed that to: *Where are you?* Juliette's English was pretty good, but maybe she wasn't so fluent in text shortcuts.

Bibliothèque, came the reply.

???? Trevor shot back.

Library, she translated. *Across the square. 3rd floor window.*

Trevor's eyes scanned the buildings on the other side of the crowded plaza. Like the square, the windows overlooking it were filled with spectators. It took him a few minutes to sift through the faces until he'd located Juliette. She waved and he acknowledged her with a small nod. The last thing he needed was to have to explain this to Dad.

Any sign of P? he texted.

Not yet. But his moto has been gone since early this morning and his mother has not seen him all day.

Trevor grimaced. So it was really happening, just like Juliette had said. Philippe was definitely going to move against G.G. during the ceremony. The only question was how.

"Are you playing a video game?" Dad whispered in annoyance. "Show some respect!"

"Sorry." Trevor slipped his phone back into his suit pocket.

The square was already jam-packed, yet still people were pouring in from the surrounding streets. At last, the mayor stepped to the podium and greeted everyone in French. Standing beside him, a younger woman translated his remarks into English for the benefit of the American guests.

"Today, we are honored to welcome one of our brightest stars. Three-quarters of a century ago, our beloved Sainte-Régine was liberated from Nazi occupation, thanks to a remarkable company of American infantrymen and their armored and artillery comrades. Their bravery and sacrifice will forever be remembered. After so many decades, all but one of these heroes has left this world . . ."

The crowd stood at attention in total silence as the mayor read the names of every soldier, artilleryman, tank crew member, and engineer who had taken part in the Battle of Sainte-Régine.

Trevor looked at his great-grandfather when the name Beauregard Howell was spoken. The old man stood a little taller, and Trevor could almost hear Beau saying, "Straighten up, High School" in one of G.G.'s endless stories. But G.G. seemed emotional at all the names, even though there were more than two hundred. These were the men he had served with, lived alongside in the mud and cold, laughed and cried with. And he had watched too many of them die. Now, to hear their names spoken and remembered in a far-off French town brought tears to his eyes.

Trevor realized that, long as it was, the list was incomplete without the names of Freddie, Leland, and the men who had lost their lives long before Bravo Company made it as far as Sainte-Régine.

Adrift in his thoughts, he almost missed the feeling of vibration against his chest.

As he pulled his phone out of his blazer, Juliette's message appeared on the screen:

He is here!

Here? Frantically, Trevor scanned the square. It was just a sea of faces, spectators listening respectfully as the names continued.

Another message buzzed in: *Pushing to the front.*

Trevor thumbed: *Where???*

In desperation, he looked to the third-floor library window just in time to see her blond head disappear from view. She was coming to try to intercept her cousin, but she'd never make it in time through this teeming humanity.

"Trev!" Dad hissed angrily, his eyes on the phone in his son's hand.

Trevor knew he was in trouble, but there was no time to

think about that now. He was on tiptoes, craning his neck, hoping to catch sight of movement in the crowd.

Juliette burst out of the library and began wading through the audience. She had seen Philippe and knew where she was going. Trevor took note of her direction and tried to project her path through the sea of people.

The mayor finished the list of names. Respectful applause filled the air.

Dad's tone was warning now, and not at all friendly. *"Trev . . ."*

"And now," the woman translated the mayor's words, "the fulfillment of our purpose here today—to present Private Jacob H. Firestone with our town's highest honor, the Order of Sainte-Régine."

The mayor reached into a velvet box and drew out a large gold medallion dangling at the end of a ribbon of the French *tricolore.*

Plowing through the crowd, Juliette leaped up, pointing wildly ahead of her in the crush of spectators.

G.G. stepped forward to receive his award. He was fully six inches taller than the mayor, and had to bow his head for the smaller man to place the ribbon around his neck.

Before, the applause had been quietly somber. Now the square resounded with a loud, joyous ovation and full-throated cheering.

And then, at the culmination of this entire trip, when the mayor backed away and G.G. stepped forward to address the citizens of Sainte-Régine, Trevor finally spotted Philippe Lafleur.

Juliette's cousin was only a couple of rows back, directly in front of the honoree. The expression on his face was carved from stone. A backpack was slung over his shoulder, and there was something shiny and metal in his hands. Trevor stood on tiptoe, straining to identify the object. And when he realized what it was, he knew panic like he had never known it before.

As G.G. opened his mouth to speak, Philippe raised the gun into clear view.

"*No!*"

The cry that was torn from Trevor's throat was barely human. Without thinking—because there was no time—he flung himself between the weapon and his great-grandfather.

CHAPTER THIRTY

SAINTE-RÉGINE, FRANCE—MAY 6

At the foot of the stage, barely six feet away, Philippe squeezed the trigger. Suddenly, Trevor's vision was filled with red. His eyes burned and he squeezed them shut.

"Trev!"

Trevor heard his father's cry and then he was squashed under Dad's weight. A second heavy blow came when G.G. jumped protectively on the two of them.

In the crowd, several spectators grabbed hold of Philippe, who dropped the gun, shouting in anger. *"Meurtrier! Meurtrier!* Murderer! I give you the blood on your hands!"

Two uniformed police officers pushed through the throng and took him into custody.

Anxiously, the mayor and some of the onstage dignitaries unpiled the Firestones and hauled them to their feet.

The mayor was babbling apologies, but no one could be heard over Dad bellowing, "Trev—are you all right?"

Trevor took stock of himself, blinking rapidly in an attempt to clear his eyes. "I'm fine, Dad."

"But you're bleeding!"

Trevor was bathed in red from head to toe. G.G. was spattered with it too. Even Dad, who'd been out of the line of fire, was smeared from his contact with his son and grandfather. Puddles of the stuff lay on the stage floor.

Trevor tasted a small drop at the corner of his mouth. "It's not blood, Dad. I think it might be *paint*."

"*La peinture?*" asked the mayor in astonishment.

One of the police officers held up Philippe's "weapon." A paint gun. The other examined the backpack. It contained a bladder of red paint connected to the gun via a plastic hose.

At this, Philippe resumed his angry shouting. Juliette pushed her way through the crowd, but she could not calm her agitated cousin. The two officers began hauling Philippe away, but at that moment, G.G. rushed to the microphone.

"Cut it out!" he barked. "Let the kid talk!"

The mayor was horrified. "But, monsieur, he is saying such terrible lies about you!"

"He's Philippe Lafleur," Trevor supplied, wiping the last of the paint out of his eyes. "René's great-grandson. And the girl is Juliette, his cousin. They're the last generation of their branch of the family."

The old soldier looked down at Philippe and Juliette. "So you know what happened. It's time that everybody knew." He addressed the crowd. "Their great-grandfather was the bravest man in all of France. The Resistance. He saved my life, and I repaid him by making the mistake that cost him his whole family. That was more than seventy-five years ago. I've lived with it that long."

He paused for a very long time, studying his shoes and struggling to regain control of his emotions. Dad tried to put an arm around his shoulders, but G.G. shook him off.

"So the kid's A-one right," he resumed. He gestured to the interpreter. "Translate so everybody understands. I'm no hero. Or maybe I am. I was here and I did the best I could, just like everybody else in my unit. We all messed up our share, and we usually got away with it. But that day, when I thought I was being G.I. Joe, I brought disaster down on a family I loved. I understand why you kids don't forgive me. I don't forgive myself. It was unforgivable."

G.G. reached under his collar and drew out a gold chain. At the end of it dangled René's metal ring. "This," he went on, "is your great-grandfather's ring. I've kept it with me ever since the last time I was in Sainte-Régine. I can't give you back your family, but you should have this."

Trevor watched in amazement as the old man hopped down from the stage. He'd been almost feeble in recent days, but all at once, he was himself again, back straight, full of vitality, no sign of the old limp. He made his way to the Lafleur cousins, pulled the chain over his head, and handed the ring to Juliette.

She stared at him for a moment, her eyes filling with tears. Then she reached out tentatively and hugged him.

Next, G.G. turned to the police officers who were holding Philippe. "How about you give the kid a break? We're not pressing charges."

The mayor nodded down to the officers, who reluctantly released Philippe's arms. The seventeen-year-old stood shamefaced next to his cousin.

The applause began slowly, then swelled to a crescendo. Soon the central square echoed with the roar of cheering.

Looking down at his great-grandfather as the ovation rolled on and on, Trevor felt his chest swelling with a kind of pride that he'd never experienced before. In that moment, he understood why it had been so important for G.G. to return to Sainte-Régine. Not to get a medal, or reminisce about blowing up a Tiger tank, but to face his past and make peace with it. The Lafleur cousins had created La Vérité to keep Private Jacob Firestone away. Yet they turned out to be the main reason he had to come. That brief embrace between G.G. and Juliette had been nothing less than a gigantic weight lifted from the old man's shoulders—one that had been crushing him for most of his long life.

Trevor shook his head in wonder. Despite its cool elements, this trip hadn't been easy. It had been horrible watching G.G. as his memories started to overwhelm him. Still, Trevor was filled with gratitude to have been a part of it all.

The mayor may have had more ceremony planned, but G.G. was already in the middle of the crowd. Hundreds of people waited patiently for the chance to shake his hand and thank the hero of Sainte-Régine. The interpreter joined him so she could translate the endless stories from the citizens—tales passed down through the generations of the Nazi occupation and the joy that liberation had brought.

Dad sidled up to Trevor, who was still wiping at the red paint on his face with a towel. "Why didn't you tell us what you knew about those two cousins?"

Trevor shrugged. "I didn't really understand until yesterday, when G.G. explained about René's family. And the poor guy was so freaked out by being back in Sainte-Régine—he didn't need to hear there was a random Lafleur out there somewhere, plotting against him. Anyway, Juliette and I thought we could handle it. I guess we were wrong about that."

Dad frowned. "You still could have told *me*."

Trevor was not ready to back down. "Like you told *me* about La Vérité?"

His father studied his paint-spattered shoes. "I thought it might scare you. I wanted you to have fun on this trip. I know I give you a hard time over your fascination with war, but it's a *good* thing to pursue your interests."

Trevor sighed. "I'm still into the war, but I've got a lot more information now. I'm not *glamorizing* it, to use your favorite word. I keep thinking about Freddie and Leland and René's family. This whole country—I mean, we liberated it, but we also blew a heck of a lot of it to smithereens."

"War makes a better video game," his father agreed. "But if you're looking for a way to live, I'll take peace every time. Now let's rescue G.G. before the locals recruit him to run for town council."

The crowd had finally thinned and the day's honoree was saying *merci* and *adieu* to the last few admirers. When they moved off, only one attendee remained—a very old man. Trevor had noticed him before, hanging back for over an hour as G.G. met with the citizens of Sainte-Régine. Now he stepped forward. He had to be about G.G.'s age, his shoulders stooped, the skin of his face wrinkled around pale blue eyes.

He said, in German-accented English, "So it *is* you."

G.G. stared. "Do I know you?"

"I would not recognize you today," the old German replied. "But when I saw your photograph as a soldier, I knew you at once. How could I forget the American who spared my life?"

"Holy—" G.G.'s jaw dropped. "You're *that* guy? Do you know how close I came to killing you?"

The man nodded fervently. "You called me 'High School.' I never forgot. I looked it up at the end of the war. You know what? You were right. I *was* in high school when they drafted me—seventeen years old!"

"No way!" G.G. exclaimed. "Me too!"

Trevor and his father watched in amazement as two mortal enemies from the deadliest conflict in human history shared a reunion as joyful as one between long-lost brothers. G.G. introduced Dad and Trevor, and the German showed photographs of his wife, their three children, seven grandchildren, and eleven great-grandchildren.

G.G. lingered over the pictures for a long time, as if he couldn't get enough of them. Trevor was confused at first. Why were these foreign strangers so important? When the answer came to him, it was like a sunrise bursting over the horizon. None of those people would have ever been born if G.G. had done his duty and killed this man so many years ago. A snap decision—a moment of mercy—and all those lives became suddenly possible.

It would not bring back René's family, but it was a miracle just the same.

CHAPTER THIRTY—ONE

MARLBOROUGH, CT—MAY 16

The rapid-fire clank of machine-gun bullets ricocheting off the armor of the Sherman tank filled the air. The driver peered through the viewfinder and located the sniper's nest, dug into the earthen mound under the base of the next hedgerow.

Trevor frowned at the video-game image on the screen in front of him. The hedgerow looked enough like the real thing. The problem was the Sherman. What was it doing here at all? Tanks were almost useless in hedgerow country. It hadn't taken the Allied commanders very long to figure that out during World War II. But whoever had designed this game either didn't know or didn't care.

Undaunted, Trevor aimed the tank's cannon at the sniper and took out the nest in a single blast. Very cool. But as he put the Sherman back in gear, he understood what was supposed to come next, and it bugged him. He was supposed to plow straight through that hedgerow into the next field. Everybody knew that the dense vegetation and root systems were too massively strong for even a Sherman to get through. He could practically hear G.G.'s voice telling the story: "The tank's stuck!"

On the other hand, this was Trevor's favorite game. He had

played this map hundreds of times. He crashed through—although he couldn't keep himself from looking away as the hedgerow disintegrated. Fat chance.

In the next field, he came under heavy fire from a German platoon. Right—like they'd just stand there in the open shooting at him when there was all this natural cover around. Didn't these game designers do research?

Suddenly, an enormous Tiger tank bulldozed through the opposite hedgerow, sixty meters away. Trevor rolled his eyes. Tigers were bigger than Shermans, but they couldn't get through hedgerows either. Still, Trevor had played this game so often that he reacted instantly. He fired two shells and watched as the enemy exploded into a million pieces. He brimmed with satisfaction, but it didn't last long. A Tiger tank wouldn't just blow apart like that. You could knock it out if the blast reached the fuel tank, but the heavy armored body would stay together.

Abandoning the tank controls, Trevor popped the hatch, took hold of the Sherman's fixed machine gun, and fired furiously down at the Germans on the ground. The room reverberated with the noise of bullets singing past his ears, some of them grazing his helmet.

The door was thrown open and Trevor's six-year-old twin half sisters stormed into the room, whooping war cries. Each brandished a Barbie doll like a submachine gun, holding on to one leg and "shooting" through the other at the video-game image on Trevor's TV screen.

"*Rat-a-tat-a-tat-a-tat!*" sang Kira.

Kelsey opted for "*Blam! Blam! Blam!*"

Trevor paused the game and leaped out of the beanbag chair to turn on the twins. "Whoa, you guys!"

"We're helping," Kira told him.

"Helping what?"

"Helping you win the war," Kelsey explained reasonably.

Trevor powered off the console, and the girls howled in protest as the image of Normandy disappeared from the TV screen.

"Listen," he said, "that's not the war. That's a video game *based* on the war. *Loosely* based," he added, picturing the Tiger tank blasting apart like a water balloon hitting the sidewalk. "It's fun to play, but it's not the real thing."

"But you *love* war," Kira protested.

The twins motioned around the room—the posters, the models of tanks and fighter planes, the action figures, the books, the school projects on every conceivable war-related subject. It certainly looked like Trevor loved war. Did he?

He definitely loved the *topic*. He would always read the books and watch the movies. He'd continue to play the video games, flaws and all. But now that he'd seen the battlefields of World War II through his great-grandfather's eyes, he knew that he didn't love war itself. It was just too awful.

His gaze found the newest picture on the wall—the one in the place of honor directly over his bed. It was a photograph Dad had taken at the last stop on their European trip. After Sainte-Régine, the Firestones had traveled to the city of Reims to attend the official ceremony marking the seventy-fifth anniversary of V-E Day—victory in Europe.

Private First Class Jacob Firestone was a guest of honor at this event too, but he was far from alone. In the picture, he stood near the front of a distinguished group of hundreds of elderly figures of all shapes, sizes, and colors who had fought together to save the world from the greatest threat it had ever faced.

Dad had always nagged Trevor about glamorizing war. But how could you not glamorize these veterans and what they had accomplished so long ago with their courage and sacrifice?

At that moment, the familiar tone of an incoming Skype call filled the room, and the TV screen displayed a photograph of a blond teenager identified as: *JULIETTE L.*

For more than seventy-five years, there had been zero contact between the Firestones and the Lafleurs, but a lot had changed in that time. Trevor and Juliette had cell phones and technology. Their long-distance friendship was off to a good start.

Kira squinted at the screen. "Who's Juliette?"

"Someone I met in France," Trevor mumbled uncomfortably.

Kelsey wouldn't leave it alone. "Is she your girlfriend?"

"Of course not! We just—had a connection."

"A *love* connection?" Kira probed.

Six wasn't as innocent as it used to be, Trevor reflected. "G.G. and her great-grandfather worked together during the war. Some bad things happened, but thanks to them, a whole town got saved."

It was a lousy explanation, but no words could ever really describe what people like G.G. had gone through during the war. Trevor had set out on this trip believing he knew it all. Now that he'd been there and seen so much, the only thing he was sure of was that he knew nothing.

He reached for the button to accept the call. "Say hello to Juliette," he told his sisters. "She's—a friend of the family."

FORT BENNING, GA—
FEBRUARY 19, 1944

The three overstuffed duffel bags stood beside the bunks, waiting for the truck to come and collect them.

"Who's got a pen?" Jacob asked.

Freddie yawned. "Do I look like Ernest Hemingway to you?"

"What do you need a pen for?" Leland added.

Jacob slapped his duffel. On the canvas was written, in blotchy ink, *FORT BENNING OR BUST.* Now they were leaving the post, their only home for months of training, shipping out for England.

"I want to cross out Fort Benning and write Berlin," Jacob explained.

Leland patted himself down. "No pen. Sorry."

Jacob shook his head sadly. "I hate to show up on Hitler's doorstep unannounced."

The barracks door flew open and another duffel was tossed inside. A second later, none other than Beau Howell ambled into the room. "Gents," he greeted the three of them.

"You better get out of here," Freddie advised the newcomer. "They're loading us up any minute now. We're shipping out."

"Yeah, me too," Beau told them.

"I thought you were a fancy paratrooper," Jacob challenged.

The big Texan shrugged. "I washed out of jump school. Fear of heights—how do you like that? You guys are Bravo, right? I'm with you now. Hope nobody snores." He regarded Jacob intently. "How old are you, kid? Shouldn't you be in high school?"

"I'm old enough," Jacob replied, knowing he wasn't.

A horn sounded outside. The truck was here to take them to a future none of them could predict. For just an instant, the steamy heat of Fort Benning turned ice-cold.

Beau gathered the four of them into a huddle. "Piece of cake, fellas. We're going to look out for each other through this whole war."

"Right," agreed seventeen-year-old Jacob Firestone. "Nothing can touch us if we stick together."

AUTHOR'S NOTE

General Eisenhower, supreme commander of the Allied Expeditionary Force in Europe during World War II, once commented, "Andrew Higgins is the man that won the war for us." Higgins's invention, the Higgins boat or LCVP (landing craft, vehicle, personnel), was the workhorse of the fleet that delivered the allied troops—like Jacob Firestone in this book—to the invasion beaches of Normandy on D-Day. Without the Higgins Boat, Eisenhower went on, "the whole strategy of the war would have been different."

One of the most fascinating details I discovered during the research for *War Stories* was that, before the war, in the 1930s, Andrew Higgins had been close to going bankrupt. He might never have stayed in business long enough to supply the boats that saved the world from the Nazis had it not been for a much shadier group of customers than the US military—American gangsters. During Prohibition, the shallow-draft Higgins boats ferried countless shipments of illegal liquor from Canada to the shores of the Great Lakes and East Coast.

To this day, the D-Day invasions stand as the largest military operation in human history. But the entire undertaking would not have been impossible without the bootleggers, rumrunners, and criminals whose support made the Higgins boat a reality. Does this make Al Capone and his associates war heroes? Of course not. What it shows is that, in a conflict as massive and chaotic as a world war, it can sometimes be difficult to tell the difference between heroics and villainy.

Behind every battle and every movement in the war, there are hundreds of stories to be found. When researching *War Stories*, I drew a lot from the reporting of war correspondents like Ernie Pyle and A. J. Liebling, accounts for adult readers like *The Longest Day* by Cornelius Ryan and *Band of Brothers* by Stephen Ambrose, and online resources like the website of the US Infantry. Among the great nonfiction resources for kids on the subject are Deborah Hopkinson's *D-Day: The World War II Invasion That Changed History* and Rick Atkinson's *D-Day: The Invasion of Normandy, 1944*. I encourage all readers to dive into the stories of World War II—and to keep in mind that the story of any war needs many voices from many sides to be fully told.